The Strange Case of
Dr. Jekyll and Mr. Hyde

The Strange Case of
Dr. Jekyll and Mr. Hyde

Robert Louis Stevenson

An Edition Prepared by
Susan J. Wolfson and Barry V. Qualls

A C O P L E Y E D I T I O N
Copley Publishing Group
Acton, Massachusetts 01720

Copley Publishing Group
138 Great Road
Acton, MA 01720
800-562-2147 • Fax 978-263-9190
email: textbook@copleypublishing.com
www.copleypublishing.com

The Editors

Susan J. Wolfson is Professor of English at Princeton University. She is the author of several critical studies of English Romantic writers, including two books, *The Questioning Presence: Wordsworth, Keats, and the Interrogative Mode in Romantic Poetry* and *Formal Charges: The Shaping of Poetry in British Romanticism*. She is also one of the editors of *The Longman Anthology of British Literature*.

Barry V. Qualls is Professor of English and Dean of Humanities at Rutgers University. He is the author of *The Secular Pilgrims of Victorian Fiction: The Novel as Book of Life* and of essays on Victorian literature and on the Bible and its literatures.

CONTENTS

Introduction

I send you herewith a Gothic gnome . . . he came out of a deep
mine, where he guards the fountain of tears. It is not always
the time to rejoice. —R.L.S., 2 January 1886

Jekyll is a dreadful thing I own; but the only thing I feel dreadful
about is that damned old business of the war in the members . . .
—R.L.S., Spring 1886

The novel, which is a work of art, exists, not by its resem-
blances to life, which are forced and material, as a shoe must
still consist of leather, but by its immeasurable difference from
life, which is designed and significant, and is both the method
and the meaning of the work.
—R.L.S., "A Humble Remonstrance" (1884)

I. ROBERT LOUIS STEVENSON: LIFE AND TIMES

The opening of MGM's 1941 film *Dr. Jekyll and Mr. Hyde* does
nearly everything that Robert Louis Stevenson was determined
that his writing *not* do. Whether the boys' stories that made his
reputation or the adult world of *Dr. Jekyll*, his novels reject the
world of Victorian domesticity—and the domestic realism that
characterized the development of the nineteenth-century English
novel. "This is a poison bad world for the romancer, this Anglo-
Saxon world," Stevenson wrote in 1892; "I usually get out of it by
not having any women in it at all." No angels in the house patrol
the moral territories of his novels; the domestic is at best a world
of proper bachelors. The film restores the moral world, opening
with an image of a church steeple and the voices of a choir
singing "The Lord Is My Shepherd." Before we ever glimpse Dr.
Jekyll and his blonde fiancée (Spencer Tracy and Lana Turner), the

rector begins to extol Victoria's Golden Jubilee year of 1887 as a sign of the ever increasing triumph of English "virtue and moral blessings" over "the forces of evil." As he intones the wonders of "family hearths" and "shops of industry" as indices of England's moral progress ("the world moves forward"), he is interrupted by an obviously lower-class man shouting that such ideas "take all the fun out of life." Dr. Jekyll goes to assist this man (his wife reports that she hoped church would help him) and finds in him the "war in the members" that Stevenson identified as his story's theme. The doctor soon experiences his own war. On the street, he meets a prostitute (Ingrid Bergman), a foil to his fiancée: the blonde angel in the house versus the whore. In his lab, he drinks a potion and becomes Mr. Hyde. Although the film surrounds these events with Freudian dream imagery and refuses to make Tracy an obvious monster when he "becomes" Hyde, it also creates the *Victorian* tale that Stevenson rejected.

Yet in essential ways, Robert Louis Stevenson (1850–1894) was a creature of this Victorian world, and it seems to have destined him to write *The Strange Case of Dr. Jekyll and Mr. Hyde*. He was the child of a prosperous Edinburgh family. His father was a High Tory (political conservative), a stern Calvinist (a believer in the perpetual antagonism of body and soul and in eternal damnation for sin), and—almost too symbolically—a lighthouse builder and civil engineer. Young Stevenson was sickly from his birth with the bronchial problems that would shadow his entire life. To calm him during his illnesses and after childhood nightmares, his father and his nurse Alison Cunningham ("Cummy") beguiled him with adventure stories. But if his father's stories calmed him, the nurse's frightened him with their fire-and-brimstone fierceness, fueled by that rigid Calvinism of a beautiful heaven and certain hell. So potent was this atmosphere in young Stevenson's life that, at age three, while drawing and playing games, he asked his mother, "I have drawed a man's *body*, shall I do his *soul* now?" and "*Why* has God got a Hell?" Of this young self, Stevenson later wrote:

> I would not only lie awake to weep for Jesus, . . . but I would fear to trust myself to slumber lest I was not accepted and should slip, ere I awoke, into eternal ruin. I remember repeatedly

. . . waking from a dream of Hell, clinging to the horizontal bar of the bed, with my knees and chin together, my soul shaken, my body convulsed with agony.

This Calvinism saturated his very identity. "A fierce underlying pessimism appears . . . to be the last word of the Stevensons," he wrote; "their sense of the tragedy of life is acute and unbroken."

The larger context for this severe, yet loving, family was the cultural and intellectual turmoil of the Victorian world. By 1850, Great Britain had entered the "age of steam" and, fueled by its Industrial Revolution, was becoming an imperialist power of Europe, indeed of the world. By 1860, it was also embroiled in heated debate over the theory of evolution advanced in Charles Darwin's *Origin of Species*. Arguing that the "natural" origin of humanity was animal and not divine, this theory posed a disturbing challenge to Victorian ideas of religious and social stability. Parallel analyses appeared during the same years from Thomas Carlyle, John Ruskin, and Karl Marx, as they described the endless fissures—and threats to our human nature—in the social foundation of modern life. In capitalist industrial society, they argued, people were not connected by human ties of fellow-feeling but set in competition by animal drives of "naked self-interest and callous cash-payment," as Carlyle put it in *Past and Present* (1843). By 1860, John Stuart Mill and Matthew Arnold were extending these arguments, tracing the tension of liberty and constraints, of culture and anarchy, agitating democratic society. By 1870, the first clearly "modern"—that is, "Godless"—writer, George Eliot, had emerged. Unlike Charles Dickens, William Thackeray, the Brontës (Charlotte, Emily, and Anne), and Elizabeth Gaskell, "she is the first great godless writer of fiction that has appeared in England," critic W. H. Mallock said in 1879:

She is the first legitimate fruit of our modern atheistic pietism. . . . For in her writings we have some sort of presentation of a world of high endeavour, pure morality, and strong enthusiasm, existing and in full work, without any reference to, or help from, the thought of God. *Godless* in its literal sense, and divested of all vindictive meaning, exactly describes her writings. They are without God, not against Him.

What seemed atheistic in Eliot's "realism" was the way she used the language of religion to represent worlds centered on human and social ties, created and sustained by a sense of duty that was not grounded in theology, or belief in divine rewards and punishment.

In the Great Britain of Stevenson's formative years, the ferment of prosperity, power, and the "march of mind" almost daily produced new ideas and new challenges to tradition. "Since yesterday, a century has passed away," says a character in Eliot's *Middlemarch*. Authority was not assumed but was up for negotiation. Even the Bible was challenged by new theories about its origins and its meanings, while long-standing political and social systems were being rattled by revolutions in Europe and workers' protests at home. To Carlyle, the "old spiritual highways and recognized paths" were obliterated. There was "no assurance of the truth of anything," said Mill. Within this ferment, and uneasily aligned with his family's fierce Scottish religious traditions, Robert Louis Stevenson tested life in what he called "the pattern of an idler." He enjoyed classes at Edinburgh University, where he started out to be an engineer, like his father, but he also found pleasure in sporadic attendance. He then studied law but really wanted only to write. Flouting the strict bourgeois respectability that meant so much to his family, he affected the style of the "dandy," sporting a velvet coat and long hair and wandering through the lowlife streets of Edinburgh, its pubs, and other haunts. He loved travel— to Italy, France, and Germany. He also had doubts about the faith of his fathers, precipitating the first great crisis of his life, in 1873, when he confessed these to his father. He loved reading—Sir Walter Scott and Alexander Dumas, Dickens and Thackeray, Poe, Hawthorne, and Whitman—and began to meet the writers and critics who would provide him a different community, particularly Sidney Colvin, Slade Professor of Art at Cambridge, who offered him enduring support as critic and friend. In France in 1876, he met Fanny Osbourne, an American woman with two children. After her divorce in 1880, they married, but marriage left him "as limp as a lady's novel," Stevenson later commented; he felt like "the embers of the once gay R.L.S."

During these years Stevenson found vitality in writing, first essays, then travel stories, poetry, adventures, and—always—

vast numbers of letters. In 1883, he published a "boy's story," *Treasure Island*. Its success and the international acclaim that greeted *Dr. Jekyll and Mr. Hyde* a few years later (1886) established his reputation. But chronic, severe bronchial problems forced him to travel to Switzerland, France, and the south of England, where he wrote *Dr. Jekyll*, as well as *Kidnapped* (also 1886). After his father's death in 1887, the family traveled to America, and then to the South Seas, settling in Samoa in 1889. Here again, Stevenson reveled in contrasts. Samoan life, he said, was "far better fun than people dream who fall asleep among the chimney stacks and telegraph wires." To the Samoans, he became "Tusitala" (teller of tales); in gratitude for his defense of them against exploitation by European and American colonists, they built a road to his house, Vailima: "The Road of Loving Hearts." He died there in 1894 of a cerebral hemorrhage while at work on *Weir of Hermiston*. The Samoans buried him at the summit of Mount Vaea.

II. THE LITERARY IMAGINATION

Alternating between "the pattern of an idler" and the industry of writing, Robert Louis Stevenson embodied the dualities that animate his poems, essays, and fiction, from children's fantasies to complex studies of adult psychological "cases." After his death, Sidney Colvin said of him,

> If you want to realize the kind of effect he made, . . . imagine this attenuated but extraordinarily vivid and vital presence, with something about it that at first struck you as freakish, rare, fantastic, a touch of the elfin and unearthly, a sprite, an Ariel. . . . He was a fellow of infinite and unrestrained jest and yet of infinite earnest, the one very often a mask for the other; a poet, an artist, an adventurer; a man beset with fleshly frailties, and despite his infirm health of strong appetites and unchecked curiosities; and yet a profoundly sincere moralist and preacher and son of the Covenanters after his fashion, deeply conscious of the war within his members, and deeply bent on acting up to the best he knew.

Colvin is alluding to Stevenson's description of the theme of *The Strange Case of Dr. Jekyll and Mr. Hyde* as the "war in the members"— a moral battle of good versus evil, a social battle of culture versus anarchy. It was shaped by the familial and intellectual conflicts that he knew from his youth and acted out in dreams. In his essay "A Chapter on Dreams" (1892), he wrote, "I had long been trying to write a story on this subject, to find a body, a vehicle, for that strong sense of man's double being which must at times come in upon and overwhelm the mind of every thinking creature." The main incidents came to him in a dream, and he wrote this "fine bogy tale" in three feverish days. But his wife felt, according to her son (who later co-wrote some stories with Stevenson), that he had "missed the allegory"; it was "merely a story—a magnificent bit of sensationalism—when it should have been a masterpiece." Stevenson burned his draft and began again, and in three more days produced *The Strange Case of Dr. Jekyll and Mr. Hyde* as we know it.

Its immediate success in England and America made Stevenson one of the celebrated writers of the *fin de siècle*. The story became so famous that its title characters are now *the* cultural emblem of a divided doubled self. Along with countless stage versions, there are three significant films, as well as comedies, farces, and cartoons featuring Stan Laurel, Abbott and Costello, Jerry Lewis and Eddie Murphy as *The Nutty Professor*, and Mighty Mouse and Bugs Bunny. There are stage musicals and prose retellings by Susan Sontag and Thomas Berger. Female versions are introduced by Emma Tennant, in *Two Women of London: The Strange Case of Ms. Jekyll and Mrs. Hyde* (1989), and in a movie titled *Dr. Jekyll and Ms. Hyde*. In 1990, novelist Valerie Martin wrote *Mary Reilly: The Untold Story of Dr. Jekyll and Mr. Hyde*, the "diary" of Dr. Jekyll's maid (a fiction), which also became a movie, starring John Malkovich and Julia Roberts.

This cultural endurance draws on a long tradition of dark doubles in the literary imagination. Prospero's words about Caliban (in Shakespeare's *The Tempest*), "This thing of darkness I/ Acknowledge mine," set the stage for the *Doppelgänger* (double) of German Romantic, English Romantic, and post-Romantic literature. The dark double descends from Faust and Macbeth, Scottish writer

James Hogg's *Confessions of a Justified Sinner* (1824), Edgar Allen Poe's "William Wilson," Nathaniel Hawthorne's *The Scarlet Letter*, and Carlyle's Diogenes Teufelsdröckh ("God-born devil's dung") from *Sartor Resartus* (1834). Carlyle, too, came from Scottish Calvinists, and all his writing is marked by a sense of doubleness and a desire for a "natural supernaturalism" as a ground for "modern" belief. "In every the wisest Soul lies a whole world of internal Madness, an authentic Demon-Empire" he wrote in *Sartor* "out of which, indeed, his world of Wisdom has been creatively built together, and now rests there, as on its dark foundations does a habitable flowery Earth-rind."

Stevenson's most important antecedent in the nineteenth century is Mary Shelley's *Frankenstein* (1818 and 1832), as reviewers noted. Her tale of science run amok, of man's nature caught between godlike and Satanic possibilities and in flight from women and domesticity (civilization, as Victorians defined it) resonates throughout his story. Her protagonist is a self-styled transgressor, a "modern Prometheus" (as her subtitle states), and a modern travesty of a divine Creator, (as the novel's epigraph from *Paradise Lost*—Adam's protest to his Creator—suggests).

Emerging from this lineage, Stevenson's novel is a hybrid: Gothic sensation and advanced science fiction, a child's nightmare and a reverse *Pilgrim's Progress* (to hell, not heaven), a Victorian novel and its antithesis, romance, but without a love story. Even its material form seemed new. It is not a typical Victorian novel, a massive work in three volumes, but a short tale printed in the mode of "sensation" novels and other "trash" books sold in railway bookstalls to readers on the run looking for entertainment rather than "literature." Yet for all its strangeness, Stevenson's novel also has a powerful appeal to ordinary, even uncannily familiar recognitions. Despite the author's repeated insistence on the novel's "immeasurable difference from life" ("Beware of realism; it is the devil," he wrote), many readers were caught by a sense a psychological realism. In one of the first reviews (January 1886), Andrew Lang thought the power of the tale derived less from its extraordinary elements than from this aura of the "ordinary":

To adopt a recent definition of some of Mr. Stevenson's tales, this little shilling work is "like Poe with the addition of a moral sense." . . . It is proof of Mr. Stevenson's skill that he has chosen the scene for his wild "Tragedy of a Body and a Soul," as it might have been called, in the most ordinary and respectable quarters of London. His heroes (surely this is original) are all middle-aged professional men. No woman appears. . . .

So mundane are these men that we almost do not notice that Stevenson, as Henry James said, always tells us less so that we may believe more. If Mrs. Stevenson feared that the "magnificent bit of sensationalism" produced in the first draft "had missed the allegory," the revision has a definite allegorical texture. Although Stevenson described his novel as a "shilling shocker," it is more: he takes the "sensation novel" that so shocked Victorians in the 1860s—for example, Mary Braddon's *Lady Audley's Secret* or Wilkie Collins's *The Woman in White*—and turns it on its head, writing an allegory of strangeness in ordinary lives. Stevenson actually made explicit what was often implicit in these shockers. Collins, Henry James noted in 1865, "introduced into fiction those most mysterious of mysteries, the mysteries which are at our own doors." Reviewing sensation novels by Braddon, Collins, and Mrs. Henry Wood, Henry Mansel suggested that the genre was really "a tale of our own times":

> Proximity is, indeed, one great element of sensation. . . . The man who shook our hand with a hearty English grasp half an hour ago—the woman whose beauty and grace were the charm of last night, and whose gentle words sent us home better pleased with the world and with ourselves—how exciting to think that under these pleasing outsides may be concealed some demon in human shape.

Within this conformity and its respectable middle-class forms, Stevenson presents "some demon in human shape."

We can see why critic Elaine Showalter crowned Stevenson "the fin-de-siècle laureate of the double life." He earned this title on the pulse of his own experience. "From his early days in Scotland till the last chapter of his life as enacted in Samoa," proposes Karl Miller (*New York Review*, 29 May 1975), "there were at least two

Stevensons: the respectable and the bohemian, the successful and the delinquent, the man of letters and the prototypical hippie." In "A Chapter on Dreams," Stevenson recalls a dream of being able to lead "a double life—one of the day, one of the night." Like his author, Dr. Jekyll reports a childhood disciplined and constrained by paternal strictures and expectations and fortified against escapist fantasies: "the days of my childhood when I walked with my father's hand." But Stevenson knows that a child's imagination may slip loose, may turn with fascination to the night life, may even invent a second self to explore it.

The poems of *A Child's Garden of Verses*—published the year that he was writing *The Strange Case of Dr. Jekyll and Mr. Hyde*—offer a symbolic biographical prelude to this "case" of a double life, as though Mr. Hyde were the adult version of the dark fantasies cultivated by the child, intuitively conscious that its deepest thrills have to stay hidden. For every "good boy," or happy child prospering in the day-world of this garden of verses, there are bad boys and children eager for, and often captivated by, nighttime adventures. With inventive imagination, the child of "Young Night Thought" describes new "people marching by / As plain as day, before my eye"— and not just once in a while, but "All night long and every night, / When my mamma puts out the light." In "Windy Nights" a child projects a mysterious adventurer into this active night:

> Whenever the moon and stars are set,
> Whenever the wind is high,
> All night long in the dark and wet,
> A man goes riding by.
> Late in the night when the fires are out,
> Why does he gallop and gallop about?

Sometimes, as in "Escape at Bedtime," adventure opens up into a world of celestial magic and glory whose shimmer is slow to leave: "the glory kept shining and bright in my eyes, / And the stars going round in my head." But just as often, the aftermath of night seems a dark haunting. The child who has voyaged to "The Land of Nod," eager for each night's return, reports perilous attractions that may prove too adhesive:

From breakfast on all through the day
At home among my friends I stay;
But every night I go abroad
Afar into the land of Nod.

All by myself I have to go,
With none to tell me what to do—
All alone beside the streams
And up the mountain-sides of dreams.

The strangest things are there for me,
Both things to eat and things to see,
And many frightening sights abroad
Till morning in the land of Nod.

Try as I like to find the way,
I never can get back by day,
Nor can remember plain and clear
The curious music that I hear.

This child seems divided between a daylight self, alienated and rest-
less among his friends in the day-world, and a night self, happily
alone and at liberty, with "none to tell [him] what to do."

Yet his is also a suspended consciousness, unable to recapture
fully, in waking life ("get back by day"), the strange, exotic, curious
night music that still plays faintly in his brain. With a more tortured
psychology, this self-division and alienation will become Dr. Jekyll's
freedom and agony. This is the implicit threat to the self-described
"Good Boy" in the *Garden of Verses*, who is a little too insistently
defensive against a denied opposite:

I woke before the morning, I was happy all the day,
I never said an ugly word, but smiled and stuck to play.

Is this a necessary discipline?

I know that, till to-morrow I shall see the sun arise,
No ugly dream shall fright my mind, no ugly sight my
        eyes . . .

The ugly dream seems an adhesive, phantom double, against whom he can't stop measuring himself. The child who tells of "Shadow March" not only has frightful sights but also believes them to have substantial agency:

> All round the house is the jet-black night;
> It stares through the window-pane;
> It crawls in the corners, hiding from the light,
> And it moves with the moving flame.
>
> Now my little heart goes a-beating like a drum,
> With the breath of the Bogie in my hair;
> And all round the candle the crooked shadows come
> And go marching along up the stair.
>
> The shadow of the balusters, the shadow of the lamp,
> The shadow of the child that goes to bed—
> All the wicked shadows coming, tramp, tramp, tramp,
> With the black night overhead.

The night that "stares" into the child's room, as if a malevolent Bogie, finds its partner in the child who casts the shadows that his heartbeat animates with "wicked" purpose. Mr. Hyde is in the lineage of this Bogie, a "bad boy" who is not quite the opposite but, rather, the spectral double of the "good boy" who wins parental approval.

In Stevenson's garden, every child seems doubled by the shadow creatures of the mind. The first poem in the subsection "The Child Alone" turns out not to be about a child alone. It is titled "The Unseen Playmate":

> When children are playing alone on the green,
> In comes the playmate that never was seen.
> When children are happy and lonely and good,
> The Friend of the Children comes out of the wood.
>
> Nobody heard him and nobody saw,
> His is a picture you never could draw,

But he's sure to be present, abroad or at home,
When children are happy and playing alone.

He lies in the laurels, he runs on the grass,
He sings when you tinkle the musical glass;
Whene'er you are happy and cannot tell why,
The Friend of the Children is sure to be by!

He loves to be little, he hates to be big,
'T is he that inhabits the caves that you dig;
'T is he when you play with your soldiers of tin
That sides with the Frenchmen and never can win.

'T is he, when at night you go off to your bed,
Bids you go to your sleep and not trouble your head;
For wherever they're lying, in cupboard or shelf,
'T is he will take care of your playthings himself!

This invisible playmate is not any one particular child's shadowy
secret but, as the poem's too-knowing voice intimates, a partner
created by all children. To say that he "inhabits the caves that you
dig" is to link him to the fundamental nature of child-play, sug-
gesting a genesis in any child's imagination, a Mr. Hyde growing
in the child's garden. "Fiction is to the grown man what play is to the
child," Stevenson wrote in his essay "A Gossip on Romance" (1882).
    In "The Child Alone," the unseen double is mostly harmless,
even at times a protective companion. But there are intimations
of Mr. Hyde in its random mischief and stubborn adolescence
("he hates to be big") and in the suggestion of a potentially transgressive energy. The unseen playmate is always siding with the
enemy (the Frenchmen), for instance, and if, in the daylight of
British internationalism, this is the losing side, the poem's last
line hints at another kind of victory: "'T is he will take care of
your playthings himself!" While you are sleeping, this double
may be a guardian caretaker, but the poem's syntax also suggests a
taking over or taking possession. Though the suggestion is oblique,
one senses Stevenson surveying the psychological terrain that he
will thicken and darken in The Strange Case of Dr. Jekyll and Mr.
Hyde. This dark antagonism is more visible in a famous poem

from *A Child's Garden of Verses*, "My Shadow," where, as in "Shadow March," a self-projection becomes the child's companion:

I have a little shadow that goes in and out with me,
And what can be the use of him is more than I can see.
He is very, very like me from the heels up to the head;
And I see him jump before me, when I jump into my bed.

The funniest thing about him is the way he likes to grow—
Not at all like proper children, which is always very slow;
For he sometimes shoots up taller like an india-rubber ball,
And he sometimes gets so little that there's none of him at all.

He hasn't got a notion of how children ought to play,
And can only make a fool of me in every sort of way.
He stays so close beside me, he's a coward you can see;
I'd think shame to stick to nursie as that shadow sticks to me!

One morning, very early, before the sun was up,
I rose and found the shining dew on every buttercup;
But my lazy little shadow, like an arrant sleepy-head,
Had stayed at home behind me and was fast asleep in bed.

This fable betrays a little more of Mr. Hyde: though not a clearly demonic presence, "my shadow" takes unpredictable forms, and though they are tied to the "me," they are also not quite subject to "me." Compared to the unseen playmate, this shadow is less controllable and overtly transgressive. "My shadow" is funny but also a little embarrassing, a little annoying in being too "like me," even a little shameful in his mimicry, and more than a little anarchic in the way that it disrupts and rebels against what is "proper" for children. It is lazy and arrant in a culture where children are raised to be industrious and obedient. What is the relationship between the "I" and this thing of darkness he acknowledges "my" own? Is this shadow most significant to the poem's speaker for being "very, very like" or for being "not at all like proper children"? The word "proper" involves this question, for it not only denotes socially desired behavior (how "children ought to" act) but also puns on the literal Latin meaning: "proper" as one's "own" ("property" is a cognate). The illogical joke in the last stanza, about the separate will of one's shadow, occurs just at the point where the speaker starts to complain about the "shame" of a shadow that "sticks to" him a little too closely.

Mary Shelley, as we noted, had explored the theme of a shadow self in *Frankenstein*. Victor Frankenstein's Creature (usually called the "Monster") is partly a separate being, not under the control of his creator (an anarchic self, released into independent life). At the same time, the symbolic structure of Shelley's novel casts this Creature as his creator's double, a being that exposes and releases into active life his darker, transgressive, violent, antisocial energies, energies that finally alienate him from human community and life itself. Popular culture reflects this doubling in its habit of using the name Frankenstein to refer to the Creature as well as to his creator. The theme of a double self is only one aspect of Shelley's complex novel (much of which solicits sympathy for the Creature as a social outcast, despised for his physical difference), but it is clearly, and darkly, the aspect that caught Stevenson's attention. Like *Frankenstein, Dr. Jekyll and Mr. Hyde* tells of a creature born from unwise, heterodox scientific experimentation, with horrific moral consequences. But Stevenson produces a critical, Victorian-era shift in psychological emphasis. In Shelley's story, Frankenstein, a student in the radical intellectual culture of late eighteenth-century Germany, is impelled by scientific idealism. He means to create an ideal being, immune to destruction by disease or ordinary physical afflictions, and flees in horror from the disappointing physical embodiment of this dream. In Stevenson's tale, Dr. Jekyll is a denizen of a late nineteenth-century England whose dominant syntax is conformity, duty, and propriety and whose economy is thus one of repression, of denying all but the most curtailed and meager indulgences of pleasure. In this world, Dr. Jekyll means to create no ideal; instead he deliberately transforms and recreates himself into an illicit Mr. Hyde in order to liberate and release a self and sensibility that he could not otherwise experience.

III. THE STRANGE CASE

With this competition of two selves in one identity, Stevenson's novel has become the most famous fable in the English language on the theme of a split personality. Dr. Jekyll describes himself (and all of us, he implies) as "two natures" or "polar twins" contending in consciousness: one desires and labors for social approval; the other rebels and labors to avoid social apprehension. A "Jekyll-and-Hyde" personality is the term bequeathed us by this tale to describe someone given to opposite, unhomogenized personalities. Although Stevenson could not have known that his characters would enter our cultural language this way, it is clear that he grasped the cultural determinant. Mr. Hyde's name, echoing the novel's recurrent vocabulary of "hid," "hidden," "secret," and "concealed," is almost too obviously devised to pun on this theme: "You have not been mad enough to hide this fellow?" cries Dr. Jekyll's lawyer, Mr. Utterson, to him.

What are the social and psychological currents that produce this hidden fellow? The sensation of "man's dual nature" is not just a metaphysical and psychological configuration, as Dr. Jekyll's summary "Statement of the Case" proposes. It is also a socially impelled formation. Stevenson writes the novel with terms that suggest that Jekyll's experiment is less a strange case of one man's amoral and antisocial science than an uncannily familiar, representative product of society itself—or, more specifically, the social contradictions and conditions that, as Jekyll puts it, "committed [him] to a profound duplicity of life" well before the idea of creating a second self occurred to him. All the contradictions that Stevenson elaborates in the world of grim, gray, proper Victorian London—between the regime of law and order and the energies of spontaneity and violence, between the devotion to work and discipline and the desire for liberty and vitality, between the commitment to respectability and the appetite for sensation—all these contradictions remain insoluble in daylight social existence, where they define and permeate a culture of propriety.

To speculate, as Dr. Jekyll has, about the possibility of separating these contradictions into distinct, unwarring entities—one proper and respectable, the other wayward and hidden from public expo- sure—is to take the measure of how fully cultural values, practices, and beliefs regulate and inhibit certain kinds of human experience, driving it underground or into alienated forms such as "Mr. Hyde." That is, Stevenson is not just writing about the polarities of personality, but also linking these polarities to, and situating them in, cultural tensions and anxieties. The war of the "polar twins" that his fable locates dramatically in Henry Jekyll is also one that his novel maps conceptually onto a larger, encompassing social world of Victorian London, where respectable daylight streets, well-polished brasses, general cleanliness, and dull Sunday walks are haunted by a nether world of back alleys, secret entrances, and cellar doorways and shadowed by the imaginary geography of "Blackmail House" and "Queer Street."

Read in terms of this dual social geography, *The Strange Case of Dr. Jekyll and Mr Hyde* is not so "strange" after all. Across the scene of his novel, we see that it is only the extremity of Dr. Jekyll's case that is "strange," not its basic contours. We sense this immediately in the way Stevenson opens the novel. He does not introduce either of the title characters; rather, we meet "Mr. Utterson the lawyer." Mr. Utterson partly functions as the framing intelligence for this strange case: he becomes its investigator, and, as his name suggests, he will be its ultimate repository, its "utterer" and heir ("son"). At the same time, his character shows the outlines of the novel's central "case." As a lawyer, Mr. Utterson is part of the social order and its determinations of right and wrong, crime and punishment, and the biblical aura of his full name, "Gabriel John Utterson," adds a suggestion of higher moral authority. But what are we to make of some of the other details that Stevenson weaves into his character? The novel opens with these sentences:

> Mr. Utterson the lawyer was a man of a rugged countenance, that was never lighted by a smile; cold, scanty and embar- rassed in discourse; backward in sentiment; lean, long, dusty, dreary, and yet somehow lovable. At friendly meetings, and when the wine was to his taste, something eminently human beaconed from his eye.

In this anatomy, Mr. Utterson (a resident of "Gaunt Street," we later find out) seems a figure more of death than of life, with one striking exception: the "rugged countenance, that was never lighted by a smile" can be lit by means of a drug, wine. With this drug, Mr. Utterson shows another self—indeed, an uncharacteristically "human" one.

Wine is a noticeably pervasive drug in the world of this novel, repeatedly represented as the agent that gives access to humanness, sentiment, and light. Mr. Utterson pours wine for Dr. Jekyll's housekeeper Mr. Poole to restore him when he is shaken by the doctor's strange and reclusive behavior; Dr. Lanyon is discovered sitting "alone over his wine." Utterson cherishes "a bottle of a particular old wine that had long dwelt unsunned in the foundations of the house." Exhuming it and sharing it with his head clerk (appropriately named Mr. Guest), Utterson is inspired to utter a kind of lyric ode to the world that wine releases into mellow being, a little land of nod in refuge from the gray fogs of the city:

> the room was gay with firelight. In the bottle the acids were long ago resolved; the imperial dye had softened with time, as the colour grows richer in stained windows; and the glow of hot autumn afternoons on hillside vineyards was ready to be set free and to disperse the fogs of London. Insensibly the lawyer melted. (p. 29)

Circumventing ordinary good sense, wine warms, melts, and sets free another reality.

Dr. Jekyll's drug, that transformative chemical potion, is not so very different in appearance and effect: "The mixture, which was at first of a reddish hue, began, in proportion as the crystals melted, to brighten in colour, to effervesce." Aside from a slight luridness and social illegitimacy, this potion seems a kind of wine. The "blood-red liquor," Dr. Jekyll says, "braced and delighted me like wine"—a giddier version of the melting warmth, the release of "something human" that Utterson experiences:

> There was something strange in my sensations, something indescribably new and, from its very novelty, incredibly sweet. I felt younger, lighter, happier in body; within I was conscious of a heady recklessness, a current of disordered sensual images running like a mill race in my fancy, a solution of the bonds of obligation, an unknown but not an innocent freedom of the soul. (p. 58)

xxvi   The Strange Case of Dr. Jekyll and Mr. Hyde

To call these effects "strange," "indescribably new," and "unknown" is to testify to the denials that shape normal social and moral behavior, not just for Jekyll but for all of London's drab professional men.

Yet there is one crucial difference between Dr. Jekyll's potion and everyone else's wine. Wine is a limited and measured indulgence, and there are no alcoholics in the world of this novel. Wine may bestow islands of warmth by firesides and in after-dinner hours, but it does not demand an ultimate "solution of the bonds of obligation." Mr. Utterson at least knows that for him, more than a little wine is a dangerous thing. Let's go back to the novel's opening. The very next thing we hear about Utterson is that "He was austere with himself; drank gin when he was alone, to mortify a taste for vintages" (wine). Utterson won't indulge his truest pleasure, but only a compromise that will "mortify"— that is, deaden—desire. In this regime of semi-denial, the significance of Mr. Hyde's having a "closet" (that is, a private room) "filled with wine" is almost too apparent. That Utterson still drinks, taking gin alone instead of wine in convivial society, exposes the contradiction of his only partial discipline. Stevenson repeats the dynamic of mortifying to describe Mr. Utterson's ambivalent fascination with Jekyll's activities. "It is one thing to mortify curiosity, another to conquer it," we hear of Utterson after he receives a strange packet signed by the late Dr. Lanyon. Mortifying a still insistent appetite is the pulse and flow of Utterson's existence. Continuing the sentence about his drinking gin instead of wine, Stevenson writes, "and though he enjoyed the theatre," Utterson "had not crossed the doors of one for twenty years." Abstention, as if from a drug that threatens addiction, is Utterson's spiritual regimen. "It was his custom" on Sunday evenings to sit with "a volume of some *dry* divinity" until midnight, "when he would go *soberly*" to bed. And no wonder: recalling some of the ills of his past conduct, he is "raised up again into a *sober* and fearful gratitude by the many that he had come so near to doing, yet avoided."

But denial is an uncertain discipline, and the contradictions erupt in the pull of temptation and the repeated trials of negotiation:

I was born in the year 18—— to a large fortune, endowed besides with excellent parts, inclined by nature to industry, fond of the respect of the wise and good among my fellow-men, and thus, as might have been supposed, with every guarantee of an honourable and distinguished future. And indeed, the worst of my faults was a certain impatient gaiety of disposition, such as has made the happiness of many, but such as I found it hard to reconcile with my imperious desire to carry my head high, and wear a more than commonly grave countenance before the public. Hence it came about that I concealed my pleasures; and that when I reached years of reflection, and began to look round me and take stock of my progress and position in the world, I stood already committed to a profound duplicity of life.

This is not Mr. Utterson's story but the opening sentences of "Henry Jekyll's Full Statement of the Case," the last chapter of Stevenson's novel. By this point, such autobiography seems more familiar than strange. Here is another inventory of proper Victorian manhood: "large fortune," "excellent parts," a character of "industry," an ethos of "respect" and social reputation. At the same time, here are admissions to "concealed pleasures," judged improper and censurable from the perspective of respectability, not trusted, but evoking "a morbid sense of shame"; here, too, is a description of a self whose "impatient gaiety" of disposition is judged a fault by a more "imperious" self, given to a discipline of cultivating an "uncommonly grave," anti-vital social persona. No wonder that puns and figures of doubleness pervade the language of Dr. Jekyll's statement, even before he comes to the reification of this doubleness in a second self: a "profound duplicity of life" is a life conducted in two worlds, each of which belies and refuses the other; "reflection" (with a primary meaning of intellectual maturity) also names the perceived doubling of the self—the sense of mirroring becoming more obvious when Dr. Jekyll says that when he looked at Mr. Hyde "in the glass, I was conscious of no repugnance, rather of a leap of welcome. This, too, was myself. In my eyes it bore a livelier image of the spirit."

This, too, is Mr. Utterson's fascination with Hyde, who stirs an intuition of this dual nature in himself. Aware of his delicate poise on the threshold between blameless and ill conduct, Utterson sometimes wonders, "almost with envy, at the high pressure of spirits" in the misdeeds of his friends and, as though they were phantoms of his own "Mr. Hyde" (grown-up versions of the naughty unseen playmates and bumptious shadows of *A Child's Garden of Verses*), he takes vicarious pleasure in their forbidden life. He does not censure their actions but develops a compromise "character" to witness their border-land and their fall into the other side: "In this character it was frequently his fortune to be the last reputable acquaintance and the last good influence in the lives of down-going men." Indeed, Utterson is the one man in the novel whose imagination is more intrigued than revolted by the presence of Mr. Hyde in his world. More than intrigued, he is "enslaved" and "haunted," as if doubling his friend Jekyll's "strange preference or bondage" to Mr. Hyde. In this fascination with Mr. Hyde, Utterson extends his vicarious pleasure (or envy) of his friends' misdeeds to recall some of his own misdeeds from "the corners of memory." And the best he can say of these ghosts is that they are "fairly blameless," yet blameworthy enough that he hopes his overall record of sobriety might balance "the many ill things he had done." Hyde has pulled something uncomfortable from the corners of consciousness, and Utterson finds himself shaping a private identity—a more extreme and proactive form of the "character" in which he maintains his acquaintance with down-going men—to accommodate this haunting: "'If he be Mr. Hyde,' he had thought, 'I shall be Mr. Seek.'"

What is Mr. Seek really seeking? Like *Frankenstein*, the novel is structured so that the reader's attention does not just move forward through the pages as we pursue a mystery (for most of us now, the suspense is not what it was for Stevenson's first readers: we know the secret of Mr. Hyde). The fictional structure of this tale is repetitive as well as linear, moving our attention back and forth—from Mr. Utterson to Mr. Hyde to Dr. Jekyll to Dr. Lanyon, and always to the city itself—as we begin to see parallels, hear echoes, and discern patterns of repetition in this world of stolid, professional, bachelor gentlemen. None of these men seeks happiness in love; none has a family or even a pet; their liberations, whether cautious or full-throttle, are not in the direction of personal intimacy or sexual pleasure. In this pattern, Dr. Jekyll's experiment comes to seem less a case of individual madness than a mirror of general social pathology. Stevenson's novel presents a vivid, fragmented, and ultimately inconclusive exploration of this pathology from several perspectives, drawing cumulative power from an intensifying, expanding panorama of the contradictions that mark late nineteenth-century social and psychological experience. Mr. Hyde cuts a shadow march through and across these contradictions, exposing the comprehensive duplicity of Victorian London.

This city itself seems both the cause of the double life of Jekyll and Hyde and an extended figure of a split self. In its world of sober professional gentlemen, the worst that one can bring upon oneself is not unhappiness but "scandal," the death of a socially viable self: name, reputation, and public credit. When Mr. Hyde is apprehended in a citizens' arrest after trampling a little girl, this is what he is threatened with, the end of his good name and connections: "We told the man we could and would make such a scandal out of this, as should make his name stink from one end of London to the other. If he had any friends or any credit, we undertook that he should lose them." Just as a "name" is a social exterior, and a good name the badge of respectability, so all the townhouses inhabited by these respectable men have proper front-door appearances. It is within this symbolic cultural grammar that we "read" the syntax of Mr. Hyde's residence, which in every detail spells a retreat from public scrutiny, denoting a region where things are hidden, are socially unacceptable. Without windows to the world and repelling all invitation (the door has neither bell nor knocker), Hyde's house bears "in every feature the marks of prolonged and sordid negligence." Its doorway hosts figures outside the patriarchal (adult, male, respectable, and professional) social order: "Tramps slouched into the recess"; children play on its steps, and schoolboys commit minor vandalism on the moldings; his street is a place of ragged children and foreign domestics seeking a morning glass of gin.

Just as these details spell what is opposite to and repressed (or kept in the back streets) by establishment proprieties, so Mr. Hyde's actions, hidden from public scrutiny, suggest repressed and alienated energies. His victims are cultural icons—an angelic girl, a benign patriarch of Parliament. The fate of the last victim, moreover, suggests another world in hiding in Victorian London, a homoerotic culture: the scene faintly suggests a horrible turn of events in a respectable MP's concealed nightlife, a miscalculated proposition turned violent, from which Utterson is quick to sense "the eddy of a scandal." When Mr. Enfield first reports to him the strange affiliation of Mr. Hyde and Dr. Jekyll, whereby Hyde is able to buy his way out of the novel's first crime, the trampling of the angel-girl, he uses darkly suggestive terms to describe Hyde's hold: "Blackmail, I suppose; an honest man paying through the nose for some of the capers of his youth. Blackmail House. . . the more it looks like Queer Street, the less I ask." "Queer" was a new word in English slang for homosexual, and blackmail was a frequent peril for its discovery (when the word "blackmail" first arose in Scotland in the sixteenth century, it was linked to such accusations). Stevenson keeps the suggestion of homosexuality as the "Mr. Hyde" of this culture implicit at best. We get no account of anyone's sex life; that much remains closeted. But the novel does present a markedly male homosocial world, in which the figure of Hyde repeatedly evokes revulsion, panic, a sense of scandal, of unnameable sins. As if mirroring a universal repressed, he produces a "loathing" and "repulsion" in those who behold him. All his witnesses agree on "the haunting sense of unexpressed deformity with which the fugitive impressed his beholders." Dr. Jekyll, speaking of himself clinically in his full statement, in the third person, writes that Hyde was an "insurgent horror . . . knit to him closer than a wife, . . . caged in his flesh." "Whereas most fiction deals with the relation between man and woman," noted the *Contemporary Review* (April 1886), "no woman's name occurs in the book, no romance is even suggested in it"; this female reviewer, Julia Wedgwood, concurred with Andrew Lang (above) about this notable feature.

These oblique suggestions of hidden, dangerously illicit life are the shadowland on which the more overt targets of Dr. Jekyll's hostility appear—the real and symbolic guardians of patriarchal social order. In his Hyde phase, Jekyll burns the letters and destroys the portrait of his father and writes "startling blasphemies" on "a copy of pious work for which Jekyll had several times expressed a great esteem." Paternal authority and its cultural enforcement and reproduction in pious works are almost magnetic targets of abuse. The long simmering of this hostility is evident in the terms in which Dr. Jekyll reviews his life: "the days of childhood, when I had walked with my father's hand" grow, as if in the control of this hand, "through the self-denying toils of my professional life." Are "kill" and "ill" significantly hidden syllables in "Jekyll"—as if Stevenson's choice of this name were designed to suggest that Hyde's killings, real and symbolic, were the activation and release of repressed rebellious desires to do ill? "I was conscious, even when I took the draught, of a more unbridled, a more furious propensity to *ill*," writes Jekyll (emphasis added). Dr. Jekyll's father is also a Jekyll. How much of Hyde's rebellion against Jekyll is Dr. Jekyll's rebellion against his Jekyll? The alter egos are a father and a son with a difference: "Jekyll had more than a father's interest" in the "pleasures and adventures of Hyde," and "Hyde had more than a son's indifference" to Jekyll's qualms and misgivings.

In the horrors of Hyde's adventures, we might read a cautionary fable: that the "Hyde" within is always an "evil," "wicked," violent self, rigorously kept in control by normative social stricture and private conscience and is liberated only at peril. Jekyll thus deploys phrases such as "ape-like fury" to describe Hyde's violent rages, and even when Hyde is repressed, Jekyll feels his presence within as a caged devil or an animal licking his chops. Hyde is violent physical energy, the Satanic enemy of reason, morality, and "the spiritual side"; he is the worst nightmare of Darwinian theory, the primitive beast lurking within the most cultured, civilized, and rational of consciousnesses. Or, as Jekyll puts it in his "Statement," aware that his very identity is on the verge of extinction, "I was slowly losing hold of my original and better self, and becoming slowly incorporated with my second and worse." This paradigm of better and worse bodes a strong moral. Whatever the initial thrills, Jekyll ultimately finds no self-completion in Mr. Hyde but instead witnesses the gradual and unstoppable erosion of his self-possession and, finally, Hyde's usurpation of his "original" identity. Such recognition shapes the last words of his statement: "Here, then, as I lay down the pen and proceed to seal up my confession, I bring the life of that unhappy Henry Jekyll to an end." The verb "seal up" suggests a self-interment, and the slide from the first person ("I") to the third person ("that unhappy Henry Jekyll") implies that Jekyll now exists only in the "statement" of writing and that the personality of the usurper Mr. Hyde is about to take over for good. Well before this final incorporation, Dr. Jekyll laments that the terrors of Mr. Hyde are "unmanning" him, and Poole (his butler) reports to Utterson that he once heard sounds from Jekyll's laboratory that seemed to be the weeping of a woman or a lost soul. Dr. Lanyon observes another form of this unmanning when he describes Jekyll's "wrestling against the approaches of the hysteria," a malady that is regarded as essentially female (a disease of the wandering womb, or *hyster*); men who lose the wrestle with hysteria implicitly lose their manliness in the defeat.

The costs are not only personal but also social: Mr. Hyde is a public danger; his effect is not to humanize and rejuvenate those with whom he comes into contact but to imperil their lives—at the very least, to bring out their worst selves. Yet the structure of social repression that haunts all the reactions to Mr. Hyde suggests that he is not reducible to any simple or final moral analysis. As in *Frankenstein*, the moral horror of the tale does not encompass its psychological and sensational interest. The licensing of Mr. Hyde is a moral caution, to be sure, but Stevenson invests him with other vital qualities—youth, health, natural enthusiasm, and adolescent rebelliousness—that invite a socio-psychological speculation. The absence, loss, or repression of these energies, not only in Dr. Jekyll but in just about everybody in proper gray London, defines their social rectitude, but the absence also seems the symptom of emotional and spiritual disease. "Smaller, slighter, and younger" than Dr. Jekyll, Mr. Hyde reanimates Jekyll's lost youth; "He was wild when he was young; a long while ago, to be sure," Utterson remembers. Jekyll's profound commitment to respectability has necessarily kept under wraps everything that is released "in the disguise of Hyde"—"the liberty, the comparative youth, the light step, leaping pulses and secret pleasures."

In this perspective, Hyde seems less a monster than a more human, more lively self seeking liberation: "I was the first that could thus plod in the public eye with a load of genial respectability, and in a moment, like a schoolboy, strip off these lendings and spring headlong into the sea of liberty." Life in the public eye is a life of moral surveillance and supervision, with its boon of respectability feeling like a slow killing burden, one that turns the pace to dull plodding under a crushing load. Jekyll's life as Hyde is a liberation from what had come to seem a fundamentally false existence, composed only of artificial lendings. With a pointed pun, he sneers at Dr. Lanyon's fastidious disapproval of his "scientific heresies" as the reaction of a "*hide*-bound pedant," as if to say that men such as the good doctor were too unimaginative to sense, let alone liberate, their own Mr. Hydes. Indeed, when Dr. Lanyon finally witnesses Jekyll's transformation into Hyde, the revelation is too much for him; it is truly mortifying. Jekyll's statement of the case presents himself as the social (even, he suggests, the human) norm, from which Lanyon's fatal hysteria, and not Jekyll's impulse for finding Mr. Hyde, seems the aberration.

The complexity of this tension between polarized selves is reflected in the overall moral irresolution of the novel. Although Dr. Jekyll renders a cautionary tale, *Dr. Jekyll and Mr. Hyde* is more than this final judgment. Stevenson presents four different points of view: Mr. Utterson's strange fascination with Hyde; Mr. Enfield's fear of probing into his mystery (his discomfort at being "surprised out of himself"—a telling phrase); Dr. Lanyon's moral disapproval of Dr. Jekyll and his inability to survive the revelation of Mr. Hyde; and finally, Dr. Jekyll's own statement of the case as his personality is on the verge of extinction by a Mr. Hyde who is no longer hidden, no longer able to be hid. Although Jekyll has the last word in the novel, its rhetorical axis leaves Mr. Utterson, like Mary Shelley's Robert Walton, in possession of the case and its several textual materials. Jekyll can refer only to a "nameless situation" and urge Utterson, the vehicle of future utterance, to "read the narrative" that Lanyon has written and then to read his own "confession." As privy to Jekyll's hidden history, Utterson becomes a second Hyde, a doubling suggested by Jekyll's rewriting of his will to name Utterson as his heir rather than Hyde. The syntax bearing this information glints with this superimposed doubling: "in the place of the name of Edward Hyde, the lawyer, with indescribable amazement, read the name of Gabriel John Utterson." As critic Garrett Stewart observes, Stevenson's word order briefly allows "Edward Hyde, the lawyer" to seem appositive, a false syntactic cue that nonetheless yields a truth about the linking of the two in Dr. Jekyll's willful secret.

As a reader of Hyde through these several narratives, Utterson is also the double of the novel's reader. Like Utterson, we are left with several texts to wonder over and assemble in our own moral self-reflection. Like Utterson, we may discover ourselves in Dr. Jekyll's strange case. "Viewed as allegory, it touches one too closely," Stevenson's friend J. A. Symonds wrote to him in March 1886; "Most of us at some epoch of our lives have been upon the verge of developing a Mr. Hyde." Symonds may have been thinking of his own homosexuality, but the sense of a hidden, forbidden self is not limited to this referent. Tortured by theological doubts and an irrepressibly sensuous imagination, Jesuit priest and poet Gerard Manley Hopkins told his friend Robert Bridges (England's poet laureate), "You are certainly wrong about Hyde being overdrawn; my Hyde is worse." Stevenson drew the connection between the textual stimulation to these self-recognitions and the chemistry that releases Mr. Hyde when he described his appetite for popular fictions (like one he would produce with *The Strange Case of Dr. Jekyll and Mr. Hyde*): "I take them like opium . . . a drug" (letter to a friend, February 1880). The Drs. Jekyll and Lanyon mark polar extremes of indulgence and inhibition, within which Utterson must figure out how to judge "Henry Jekyll's Full Statement of the Case"—not as a lawyer, but as a sympathetic fellow human being. "Judge for yourself" is Dr. Jekyll's plea to Dr. Lanyon. Utterson is the heir to this challenge, and so are we.

Susan Wolfson
Barry Qualls

A Note on the Text

We used the first edition of 1886, published by Longman, Green. This firm actually issued the novel in two alter-ego forms (as critic Elaine Showalter tropes them), a respectable Dr. Jekyll-like clothbound voulme and a Hyde-like shilling shocker.

The Strange Case of
Dr. Jekyll and Mr. Hyde

To
Katharine de Mattos*

It's ill to loose the bands that God decreed to bind;
Still will we be the children of the heather
and the wind;
Far away from home, O it's still for you and me
That the broom is blowing bonnie in the
north countrie.

*Katharine de Mattos was a favorite cousin. Stevenson dedicated two other poems to her in *Underwoods* and wrote these lines specifically for this dedication.

1

Story of the Door

Mr. Utterson the lawyer was a man of a rugged countenance, that was never lighted by a smile; cold, scanty and embarrassed in discourse; backward in sentiment; lean, long, dusty, dreary, and yet somehow lovable. At friendly meetings, when the wine was to his taste, something eminently human beaconed from his eye; something indeed which never found its way into his talk, but which spoke not only in these silent symbols of the after-dinner face, but more often and loudly in the acts of his life. He was austere with himself; drank gin when he was alone, to mortify a taste for vintages; and though he enjoyed the theatre, had not crossed the doors of one for twenty years. But he had an approved tolerance for others; sometimes wondering, almost with envy, at the high pressure of spirits involved in their misdeeds; and in any extremity inclined to help rather than to reprove. "I incline to Cain's heresy,"[1] he used to say quaintly: "I let my brother go to the devil in his own way." In this character it was frequently his fortune to be the last reputable acquaintance and the last good influence in the lives of down-going men. And to such as these, so long as they came about his chambers, he never marked a shade of change in his demeanour.

No doubt the feat was easy to Mr. Utterson; for he was undemonstrative at the best, and even his friendships seemed to be founded in a similar catholicity of good-nature. It is the mark of a modest man to accept his friendly circle ready made from the hands of opportunity; and that was the lawyer's way. His friends were those of his own blood, or those whom he had known the longest; his affections, like ivy, were the growth of time, they implied no aptness in the object. Hence, no doubt, the bond that united him to Mr. Richard Enfield, his distant kinsman, the well-known man about town. It was a nut to crack for many, what these two could see in each other, or what subject they could find in common. It was reported by those who encountered them in their Sunday walks, that they said nothing, looked singularly dull, and would hail with obvious relief the appearance of a friend. For all that, the two men put the greatest store by these excursions, counted them the chief jewel of each week, and not only set aside occasions of pleasure, but even resisted the calls of business, that they might enjoy them uninterrupted.

It chanced on one of these rambles that their way led them down a by street in a busy quarter of London. The street was small and what is called quiet, but it drove a thriving trade on the week-days. The inhabitants were all doing well, it seemed, and all emulously hoping to do better still, and laying out the surplus of their gains in coquetry; so that the shop fronts stood along that thoroughfare with an air of invitation, like rows of smiling sales-women. Even on Sunday, when it veiled its more florid charms and lay comparatively empty of passage, the street shone out in contrast to its dingy neighbourhood, like a fire in a forest; and with its freshly painted shutters, well-polished brasses, and general cleanliness and gaiety of note, instantly caught and pleased the eye of the passenger.

Two doors from one corner, on the left hand going east, the line was broken by the entry of a court; and just at that point, a certain sinister block of building thrust forward its gable on the street. It was two storeys high; showed no window, nothing but a door on the lower storey and a blind forehead of discoloured wall on the upper; and bore in every feature the marks of prolonged and sordid negligence. The door, which was equipped with neither bell nor knocker, was blistered and distained. Tramps slouched into the recess and struck matches on the panels; children kept shop upon the steps; the schoolboy had tried his knife on the mouldings; and for close on a generation no one had appeared to drive away these random visitors or to repair their ravages.

Mr. Enfield and the lawyer were on the other side of the by street; but when they came abreast of the entry, the former lifted up his cane and pointed.

"Did you ever remark that door?" he asked; and when his companion had replied in the affirmative, "It is connected in my mind," added he, "with a very odd story."

"Indeed!" said Mr. Utterson, with a slight change of voice, "and what was that?"

"Well, it was this way," returned Mr. Enfield: "I was coming home from some place at the end of the world, about three o'clock of a black winter morning, and my way lay through a part of town where there was literally nothing to be seen but lamps. Street after street, and all the folks asleep—street after street, all lighted up as if for a procession, and all as empty as a church—till at last I got into that state of mind when a man listens and listens and begins to long for the sight of a policeman. All at once, I saw two figures: one a little man who was stumping along eastward at a good walk, and the other a girl of maybe eight or ten who was running as hard as she was able down a cross-street. Well, sir, the two ran into one another naturally enough at the corner; and then came the horrible part of the thing; for the man trampled calmly over the child's body and left her screaming on the ground. It sounds nothing to hear, but it was hellish to see. It wasn't like a man; it was like some damned Juggernaut.[2] I gave a view halloa, took to my heels, collared my gentleman, and brought him back to where there was already quite a group about the screaming child. He was perfectly cool and made no resistance, but gave me one look, so ugly that it brought out the sweat on me like running. The people who had turned out were the girl's own family; and pretty soon the doctor, for whom she had been sent, put in his appearance. Well, the child was not much the worse, more frightened, according to the Sawbones; and there you might have supposed would be an end to it. But there was one curious circumstance. I had taken a loathing to my gentleman at first sight. So had the child's family, which was only natural. But the doctor's case was what struck me. He was the usual cut-and-dry apothecary, of no particular age and colour, with a strong Edinburgh accent, and about as emotional as a bagpipe. Well, sir, he was like the rest of us: every time he looked at my prisoner, I saw that Sawbones turned sick and white with the desire to kill him. I knew what was in his mind, just as he knew

what was in mine; and killing being out of the question, we did
the next best. We told the man we could and would make such a
scandal out of this, as should make his name stink from one end
of London to the other. If he had any friends or any credit, we
undertook that he should lose them. And all the time, as we were
pitching it in red hot, we were keeping the women off him as best
we could, for they were as wild as harpies. I never saw a circle of
such hateful faces; and there was the man in the middle, with a
kind of black sneering coolness—frightened too, I could see
that—but carrying it off, sir, really like Satan. 'If you choose to
make capital out of this accident,' said he, 'I am naturally helpless.
No gentleman but wishes to avoid a scene,' says he, 'Name your
figure.' Well, we screwed him up to a hundred pounds for the
child's family; he would have clearly liked to stick out; but there
was something about the lot of us that meant mischief, and at last
he struck. The next thing was to get the money; and where do
you think he carried us but to that place with the door?—
whipped out a key, went in, and presently came back with the
matter of ten pounds in gold and a cheque for the balance on
Coutts's,[3] drawn payable to bearer, and signed with a name that
I can't mention, though it's one of the points of my story, but it
was a name at least very well known and often printed. The figure
was stiff, but the signature was good for more than that, if it was
only genuine. I took the liberty of pointing out to my gentleman
that the whole business looked apocryphal; and that a man does
not, in real life, walk into a cellar door at four in the morning and
come out of it with another man's cheque for close upon a hundred
pounds. But he was quite easy and sneering. 'Set your mind at
rest,' says he, 'I will stay with you till the banks open, and cash
the cheque myself.' So we all set off, the doctor, and the child's
father, and our friend and myself, and passed the rest of the night
in my chambers; and next day, when we had breakfasted, went
in a body to the bank. I gave in the cheque myself, and said I had
every reason to believe it was a forgery. Not a bit of it. The cheque
was genuine."

"Tut-tut!" said Mr. Utterson.

"I see you feel as I do," said Mr. Enfield. "Yes, it's a bad story.
For my man was a fellow that nobody could have to do with, a

really damnable man; and the person that drew the cheque is the very pink of the proprieties, celebrated too, and (what makes it worse) one of your fellows who do what they call good. Blackmail, I suppose; an honest man paying through the nose for some of the capers of his youth. Blackmail House is what I call that place with the door, in consequence. Though even that, you know, is far from explaining all," he added; and with the words fell into a vein of musing.

From this he was recalled by Mr. Utterson asking rather suddenly: "And you don't know if the drawer of the cheque lives there?"

"A likely place, isn't it?" returned Mr. Enfield. "But I happen to have noticed his address; he lives in some square or other."

"And you never asked about—the place with the door?" said Mr. Utterson.

"No, sir: I had a delicacy," was the reply. "I feel very strongly about putting questions; it partakes too much of the style of the day of judgment. You start a question, and it's like starting a stone. You sit quietly on the top of a hill; and away the stone goes, starting others; and presently some bland old bird (the last you would have thought of) is knocked on the head in his own back garden, and the family have to change their name. No, sir, I make it a rule of mine: the more it looks like Queer Street,[4] the less I ask."

"A very good rule, too," said the lawyer.

"But I have studied the place for myself," continued Mr. Enfield. "It seems scarcely a house. There is no other door, and nobody goes in or out of that one, but, once in a great while, the gentleman of my adventure. There are three windows looking on the court on the first floor; none below; the windows are always shut, but they're clean. And then there is a chimney, which is generally smoking; so somebody must live there. And yet it's not so sure; for the buildings are so packed together about that court, that it's hard to say where one ends and another begins."

The pair walked on again for a while in silence; and then— "Enfield," said Mr. Utterson, "that's a good rule of yours."

"Yes, I think it is," returned Enfield.

"But for all that," continued the lawyer, "there's one point I want to ask: I want to ask the name of that man who walked over the child."

"Well," said Mr. Enfield, "I can't see what harm it would do. It was a man of the name of Hyde."

"Hm," said Mr. Utterson. "What sort of a man is he to see?"

"He is not easy to describe. There is something wrong with his appearance; something displeasing, something downright detestable. I never saw a man I so disliked, and yet I scarce know why. He must be deformed somewhere; he gives a strong feeling of deformity, although I couldn't specify the point. He's an extraordinary-looking man, and yet I really can name nothing out of the way. No, sir; I can make no hand of it; I can't describe him. And it's not want of memory; for I declare I can see him this moment."

Mr. Utterson again walked some way in silence, and obviously under a weight of consideration. "You are sure he used a key?" he inquired at last.

"My dear sir . . ." began Enfield, surprised out of himself.

"Yes, I know," said Utterson; "I know it must seem strange. The fact is, if I do not ask you the name of the other party, it is because I know it already. You see, Richard, your tale has gone home. If you have been inexact in any point, you had better correct it."

"I think you might have warned me," returned the other, with a touch of sullenness. "But I have been pedantically exact, as you call it. The fellow had a key; and, what's more, he has it still. I saw him use it, not a week ago."

Mr. Utterson sighed deeply, but said never a word; and the young man presently resumed. "Here is another lesson to say nothing," said he. "I am ashamed of my long tongue. Let us make a bargain never to refer to this again."

"With all my heart," said the lawyer. "I shake hands on that, Richard."

Notes

[1] Cain's retort to the Lord's question about the whereabouts of his brother Abel, whom he has murdered in a fit of jealousy (*Genesis* 4.8–15): And the Lord said unto Cain, "Where is Abel thy brother?" And he said, "I know not: Am I my brother's keeper?"

[2] From "Jagannath," the Hindi title of the eighth avatar of the god Vishnu (literally "Lord of the world" [*Jaga*: world + *natha*: protector]), *juggernaut* is the icon of an all-destroying, inexorable force. In India, an idol of this deity was dragged annually in procession on a huge chariot, and devotees are said to have thrown themselves in front of it, to be crushed to death. Reports of this ritual entered England in the late 1300s and were still being circulated in the nineteenth century.

[3] A major English bank.

[4] Slang for an embarrassing situation, especially of financial difficulty. Charles Dickens used the term in *Our Mutual Friend* (1865): "Queer Street is full of lodgers just at present."

Search for Mr. Hyde

That evening Mr. Utterson came home to his bachelor house in sombre spirits, and sat down to dinner without relish. It was his custom of a Sunday, when this meal was over, to sit close by the fire, a volume of some dry divinity on his reading-desk, until the clock of the neighbouring church rang out the hour of twelve, when he would go soberly and gratefully to bed. On this night, however, as soon as the cloth was taken away, he took up a candle and went into his business room. There he opened his safe, took from the most private part of it a document endorsed on the envelope as Dr. Jekyll's Will, and sat down with a clouded brow to study its contents. The will was holograph; for Mr. Utterson, though he took charge of it now that it was made, had refused to lend the least assistance in the making of it; it provided not only that, in case of the decease of Henry Jekyll, M.D., D.C.L., LL.D., F.R.S.,[1] &c., all his possessions were to pass into the hands of his "friend and benefactor Edward Hyde"; but that in case of Dr. Jekyll's "disappearance or unexplained absence for any period exceeding three calendar months," the said Edward Hyde should step into the said Henry Jekyll's shoes without further delay, and free from any burthen or obligation, beyond the payment of a few small sums to the members of the doctor's household. This document had long been the lawyer's eyesore. It offended him both as a lawyer and as a lover of the sane and customary sides of life, to whom the fanciful was the immodest. And hitherto it was his ignorance of Mr. Hyde that had swelled his indignation; now, by a sudden turn, it was his knowledge. It was already bad enough when the name was but a name of which he could learn no more. It was worse when it began to be clothed upon with detestable attributes; and out of the shifting, insubstantial mists that had so long baffled his eye, there leaped up the sudden, definite presentment of a fiend.

"I thought it was madness," he said, as he replaced the obnoxious paper in the safe; "and now I begin to fear it is disgrace."

With that he blew out his candle, put on a great coat, and set forth in the direction of Cavendish Square, that citadel of medicine, where his friend the great Dr. Lanyon, had his house and received his crowding patients. "If any one knows, it will be Lanyon," he had thought.

The solemn butler knew and welcomed him; he was subjected to no stage of delay, but ushered direct from the door to the dining room, where Dr. Lanyon sat alone over his wine. This was a hearty, healthy, dapper, red-faced gentleman, with a shock of hair prematurely white, and a boisterous and decided manner. At sight of Mr. Utterson, he sprang up from his chair and welcomed him with both hands. The geniality, as was the way of the man, was somewhat theatrical to the eye; but it reposed on genuine feeling. For these two were old friends, old mates both at school and college, both thorough respecters of themselves and of each other, and, what does not always follow, men who thoroughly enjoyed each other's company.

After a little rambling talk, the lawyer led up to the subject which so disagreeably preoccupied his mind.

"I suppose, Lanyon," he said, "you and I must be the two oldest friends that Henry Jekyll has?"

"I wish the friends were younger," chuckled Dr. Lanyon. "But I suppose we are. And what of that? I see little of him now."

"Indeed!" said Utterson. "I thought you had a bond of common interest."

"We had," was his reply. "But it is more than ten years since Henry Jekyll became too fanciful for me. He began to go wrong, wrong in mind; and though, of course, I continue to take an interest in him for old sake's sake as they say, I see and I have seen devilish little of the man. Such unscientific balderdash," added the doctor, flushing suddenly purple, "would have estranged Damon and Pythias."[2]

This little spirt of temper was somewhat of a relief to Mr. Utterson. "They have only differed on some point of science," he thought; and being a man of no scientific passions (except in the matter of conveyancing),[3] he even added: "It is nothing worse than that!" He gave his friend a few seconds to recover his composure, and then approached the question he had come to put.

"Did you ever come across a *protégé* [4] of his—one Hyde?" he asked.

"Hyde?" repeated Lanyon. "No. Never heard of him. Since my time."

That was the amount of information that the lawyer carried back with him to the great, dark bed on which he tossed to and fro until the small hours of the morning began to grow large. It was a night of little ease to his toiling mind, toiling in mere darkness and besieged by questions.

Six o'clock struck on the bells of the church that was so conveniently near to Mr. Utterson's dwelling, and still he was digging at the problem. Hitherto it had touched him on the intellectual side alone; but now his imagination also was engaged, or rather enslaved; and as he lay and tossed in the gross darkness of the night and the curtained room, Mr. Enfield's tale went by before his mind in a scroll of lighted pictures. He would be aware of the great field of lamps of a nocturnal city; then of the figure of a man walking swiftly; then of a child running from the doctor's; and then these met, and that human Juggernaut trod the child down and passed on regardless of her screams. Or else he would see a room in a rich house, where his friend lay asleep, dreaming and smiling at his dreams; and then the door of that room would be opened, the curtains of the bed plucked apart, the sleeper recalled, and, lo! there would stand by his side a figure to whom power was given, and even at that dead hour he must rise and do its bidding.[5] The figure in these two phases haunted the lawyer all night; and if at any time he dozed over, it was but to see it glide more stealthily through sleeping houses, or move the more swiftly, and still the more swiftly, even to dizziness, through wider labyrinths of lamp-lighted city, and at every street corner crush a child and leave her screaming. And still the figure had no face by which he might know it; even in his dreams it had no face, or one that baffled him and melted before his eyes; and thus it was that there sprang up and grew apace in the lawyer's mind a singularly strong, almost an inordinate, curiosity to behold the features of the real Mr. Hyde. If he could but once set eyes on him, he thought the mystery would lighten and perhaps roll altogether away, as was the habit of mysterious things when well examined. He might see a reason for his friend's strange preference or bondage (call it which you please), and even for the startling clauses of the will. And at least it would be a face worth seeing: the face of a man who was without bowels of mercy: a face which had but to show itself to raise up, in the mind of the unimpressionable Enfield, a spirit of enduring hatred.

From that time forward, Mr. Utterson began to haunt the door in the by street of shops. In the morning before office hours, at noon when business was plenty and time scarce, at night under the face of the fogged city moon, by all lights and at all hours of solitude or concourse, the lawyer was to be found on his chosen post.

"If he be Mr. Hyde," he had thought, "I shall be Mr. Seek."

And at last his patience was rewarded. It was a fine dry night; frost in the air; the streets as clean as a ballroom floor; the lamps, unshaken by any wind, drawing a regular pattern of light and shadow. By ten o'clock, when the shops were closed, the by street was very solitary, and, in spite of the low growl of London from all around, very silent. Small sounds carried far; domestic sounds out of the houses were clearly audible on either side of the roadway; and the rumour of the approach of any passenger preceded him by a long time. Mr. Utterson had been some minutes at his post when he was aware of an odd light footstep drawing near. In the course of his nightly patrols he had long grown accustomed to the quaint effect with which the footfalls of a single person, while he is still a great way off, suddenly spring out distinct from the vast hum and clatter of the city. Yet his attention had never before been so sharply and decisively arrested: and it was with a strong, superstitious pre-vision of success that he withdrew into the entry of the court.

The steps drew swiftly nearer, and swelled out suddenly louder as they turned the end of the street. The lawyer, looking forth from the entry, could soon see what manner of man he had to deal with. He was small, and very plainly dressed; and the look of him, even at that distance, went somehow strongly against the watcher's inclination. But he made straight for the door, crossing the roadway to save time; and as he came, he drew a key from his pocket, like one approaching home.

Mr. Utterson stepped out and touched him on the shoulder as he passed. "Mr. Hyde, I think?"

Mr. Hyde shrank back with a hissing intake of the breath. But his fear was only momentary; and though he did not look the lawyer in the face, he answered coolly enough: "That is my name. What do you want?"

"I see you are going in," returned the lawyer. "I am an old friend of Dr. Jekyll's,—Mr. Utterson, of Gaunt Street—you must have heard my name; and meeting you so conveniently, I thought you might admit me."

"You will not find Dr. Jekyll; he is from home," replied Mr. Hyde, blowing in the key. And then suddenly, but still without looking up, "How did you know me?" he asked.

"On your side," said Mr. Utterson, "will you do me a favour?"

"With pleasure," replied the other. "What shall it be?"

"Will you let me see your face?" asked the lawyer.

Mr. Hyde appeared to hesitate; and then, as if upon some sudden reflection, fronted about with an air of defiance; and the pair stared at each other pretty fixedly for a few seconds. "Now I shall know you again," said Mr. Utterson. "It may be useful."

"Yes," returned Mr. Hyde, "it is as well we have met; and *à propos*, you should have my address." And he gave a number of a street in Soho.⁶

"Good God!" thought Mr. Utterson, "can he too have been thinking of the will?" But he kept his feelings to himself, and only grunted in acknowledgment of the address.

"And now," said the other, "how did you know me?"

"By description," was the reply.

"Whose description?"

"We have common friends," said Mr. Utterson.

"Common friends!" echoed Mr. Hyde, a little hoarsely. "Who are they?"

"Jekyll, for instance," said the lawyer.

"He never told you," cried Mr. Hyde, with a flush of anger. "I did not think you would have lied."

"Come," said Mr. Utterson, "that is not fitting language."

The other snarled aloud into a savage laugh; and the next moment, with extraordinary quickness, he had unlocked the door and disappeared into the house.

The lawyer stood awhile when Mr. Hyde had left him, the picture of disquietude. Then he began slowly to mount the street, pausing every step or two, and putting his hand to his brow like a man in mental perplexity. The problem he was thus debating as he walked was one of a class that is rarely solved. Mr. Hyde was pale and dwarfish; he gave an impression of deformity without any namable malformation, he had a displeasing smile, he had borne himself to the lawyer with a sort of murderous mixture of timidity and boldness, and he spoke with a husky, whispering and somewhat broken voice,—all these were points against him; but not all of these together could explain the hitherto unknown disgust, loathing and fear with which Mr. Utterson regarded him. "There must be something else," said the perplexed gentleman. "There *is* something more, if I could find a name for it. God bless me, the man seems hardly human! Something troglodytic,[7] shall we say? or can it be the old story of Dr. Fell?[8] or is it the mere radiance of a foul soul that thus transpires through, and transfigures, its clay continent? The last, I think; for, O my poor old Harry[9] Jekyll, if ever I read Satan's signature upon a face, it is on that of your new friend!"

Round the corner from the by street there was a square of ancient, handsome houses, now for the most part decayed from their high estate, and let in flats and chambers to all sorts and conditions of men: map-engravers, architects, shady lawyers, and the agents of obscure enterprises. One house, however, second from the corner, was still occupied entire; and at the door of this, which wore a great air of wealth and comfort, though it was now plunged in darkness except for the fan-light, Mr. Utterson stopped and knocked. A well-dressed, elderly servant opened the door.

"Is Dr. Jekyll at home, Poole?"[10] asked the lawyer.

"I will see, Mr. Utterson," said Poole, admitting the visitor, as he spoke, into a large, low-roofed, comfortable hall, paved with flags, warmed (after the fashion of a country house) by a bright, open fire, and furnished with costly cabinets of oak. "Will you wait here by the fire, sir? or shall I give you a light in the dining-room?"

"Here, thank you," said the lawyer; and he drew near and leaned on the tall fender. This hall, in which he was now left alone, was a pet fancy of his friend the doctor's; and Utterson himself was wont to speak of it as the pleasantest room in London. But to-night there was a shudder in his blood; the face of Hyde sat heavy on his memory; he felt (what was rare in him) a nausea and distaste of life; and in the gloom of his spirits, he seemed to read a menace in the flickering of the firelight on the polished cabinets and the uneasy starting of the shadow on the roof. He was ashamed of his relief when Poole presently returned to announce that Dr. Jekyll was gone out.

"I saw Mr. Hyde go in by the old dissecting-room door, Poole," he said. "Is that right, when Dr. Jekyll is from home?"

"Quite right, Mr. Utterson, sir," replied the servant. "Mr. Hyde has a key."

"Your master seems to repose a great deal of trust in that young man, Poole," resumed the other, musingly.

"Yes, sir, he do indeed," said Poole. "We have all orders to obey him."

"I do not think I ever met Mr. Hyde?" asked Utterson.

"O dear no, sir. He never *dines* here," replied the butler. "Indeed, we see very little of him on this side of the house; he mostly comes and goes by the laboratory."

"Well, good-night, Poole."

"Good-night, Mr. Utterson."

And the lawyer set out homeward with a very heavy heart. "Poor Harry Jekyll," he thought, "my mind misgives me he is in deep waters! He was wild when he was young; a long while ago, to be sure; but in the law of God there is no statute of limitations. Ah, it must be that; the ghost of some old sin, the cancer of some concealed disgrace; punishment coming, *pede claudo*,[11] years after memory has forgotten and self-love condoned the fault." And the lawyer, scared by the thought, brooded awhile on his own past, groping in all the corners of memory, lest by chance some Jack-in-the-Box of an old iniquity should leap to light there. His past was fairly blameless; few men could read the rolls of their life with less apprehension; yet he was humbled to the dust by the many ill things he had done, and raised up again into a sober and fearful gratitude by the many that he had come so near to doing, yet avoided. And then by a return on his former subject, he conceived a spark of hope. "This Master Hyde, if he were studied," thought he, "must have secrets of his own: black secrets, by the look of him; secrets compared to which poor Jekyll's worst would be like sunshine. Things cannot continue as they are. It turns me quite cold to think of this creature stealing like a thief to Harry's bedside; poor Harry, what a wakening! And the danger of it! for if this Hyde suspects the existence of the will, he may grow impatient to inherit. Ay, I must put my shoulder to the wheel—if Jekyll will but let me," he added, "if Jekyll will only let me." For once more he saw before his mind's eye, as clear as a transparency, the strange clauses of the will.

Notes

[1] Professional credentials: Medical Doctor, Doctor of Civil Law, Doctor of Law, Fellow of the Royal Society (for scientists).

[2] These two young men in Greek legend epitomized loyal friendship. In the first half of the fourth century B.C., when Pythagoreans Damon and Pythias visited Syracuse, Pythias was arrested on trumped-up charges of spying and conspiracy against the tyrant, Dionysius, who sentenced him to death. Dionysius allowed him to return home to settle his affairs first, holding Damon in security for his return. When Pythias's return was unexpectedly delayed, Damon was turned over for execution but was saved by the last-minute arrival of Pythias. Witnessing each friend strive to save the other by volunteering for death, Dionysius was so impressed that he pardoned both.

[3] The drawing up of deeds and other legal documents for the transfer of property from one person to another, and, more generally, legal practice devoted to these matters; *conveyancing* may also refer to the fraudulent transfer of property or swindling, recovering the obsolete sense (which Utterson means) of sleight of hand, deceitful or underhanded practices.

[4] One under the protection (more generally, the sponsorship) of another.

[5] Stevenson recalls a famous scene in Mary Shelley's *Frankenstein*, another tale of unlawful scientific experimentation. Victor Frankenstein has run out of the laboratory, horrified at his creation, and faints away into sleep, which is then interrupted by his "monster": "by the dim and yellow light of the moon, as it forced its way through the window-shutters, I beheld the wretch—the miserable monster whom I had created. He held up the curtain of the bed; and his eyes, if eyes they may be called, were fixed on me . . . one hand was stretched out, seemingly to detain me."

[6] Once a fashionable district of London, but by the nineteenth century an arty, literary, colorful, and somewhat disreputable part of town.

[7] Unsocialized, reclusive, unworldly. The adjective is derived from the Greek *trogle* (hole, cave) and *dyein* (to enter), originally referring to primitive cave dwellers. This etymology evokes that "unseen playmate" in the poem from *A Child's Garden of Verses* who "inhabits the caves that you dig" and hits the Darwinian theme of this novel: the primitive self within, or just beneath, the surface of civilization. "Perhaps we shall not be far wrong if we regard Troglodytism as the primitive state of all mankind" (*Chambers' Encyclopedia*, 1867).

[8] Dr. John Fell (1625–1686), an English doctor, prelate, dean of Christ Church, Oxford, promised to cancel a sentence of expulsion on Thomas Brown (1663–1704) if Brown could provide an extempore translation of Martial's 23rd epigram: "Non amo te, Sabidi, nec possum dicere quare; / Hoc tantum possum non amo te" [I do not love you, Sabidi, nor can I say why; / This much I can—I do not love you]. Brown's quatrain became famous: "I do not love thee Dr. Fell, / The reason why I cannot tell; / But this I know, and know full well, / I do not love thee Dr. Fell."

[9] Though said with compassion, *old Harry* is standard slang for the devil, a sense Utterson evokes when he describes Hyde in the same sentence as bearing "Satan's signature" on his face.

[10] The name *Poole* evokes "Grace Poole" of Charlotte Brontë's *Jane Eyre* (1847), the warden of Bertha Mason, Edward Rochester's mad wife, secretly lodged in the attic of Thornfield Hall.

[11] Latin for "on halting foot"—the way past sins slowly but inexorably catch up with one.

Dr. Jekyll Was Quite at Ease

A fortnight later, by excellent good fortune, the doctor gave one of his pleasant dinners to some five or six old cronies, all intelligent reputable men, and all judges of good wine; and Mr. Utterson so contrived that he remained behind after the others had departed. This was no new arrangement, but a thing that had befallen many scores of times. Where Utterson was liked, he was liked well. Hosts loved to detain the dry lawyer, when the light-hearted and the loose-tongued had already their foot on the threshold; they liked to sit awhile in his unobtrusive company, practising for solitude, sobering their minds in the man's rich silence, after the expense and strain of gaiety. To this rule Dr. Jekyll was no exception; and as he now sat on the opposite side of the fire—a large, well-made, smooth-faced man of fifty, with something of a slyish cast perhaps, but every mark of capacity and kindness—you could see by his looks that he cherished for Mr. Utterson a sincere and warm affection.

"I have been wanting to speak to you, Jekyll," began the latter. "You know that will of yours?"

A close observer might have gathered that the topic was distasteful; but the doctor carried it off gaily. "My poor Utterson," said he, "you are unfortunate in such a client. I never saw a man so distressed as you were by my will; unless it were that hide-bound pedant, Lanyon, at what he called my scientific heresies. O, I know he's a good fellow—you needn't frown—an excellent fellow, and I always mean to see more of him; but a hide-bound pedant for all that; an ignorant, blatant pedant. I was never more disappointed in any man than Lanyon."

"You know I never approved of it," pursued Utterson, ruthlessly disregarding the fresh topic.

"My will? Yes, certainly, I know that," said the doctor, a trifle sharply. "You have told me so."

"Well, I tell you so again," continued the lawyer. "I have been learning something of young Hyde."

The large handsome face of Dr. Jekyll grew pale to the very lips, and there came a blackness about his eyes. "I do not care to hear more," said he. "This is a matter I thought we had agreed to drop."

"What I heard was abominable," said Utterson.

"It can make no change. You do not understand my position," returned the doctor, with a certain incoherency of manner. "I am painfully situated, Utterson; my position is a very strange—a very strange one. It is one of those affairs that cannot be mended by talking."

"Jekyll," said Utterson, "you know me: I am a man to be trusted. Make a clean breast of this in confidence; and I make no doubt I can get you out of it."

"My good Utterson," said the doctor, "this is very good of you, this is downright good of you, and I cannot find words to thank you in. I believe you fully; I would trust you before any man alive, ay, before myself, if I could make the choice; but indeed it isn't what you fancy; it is not so bad as that; and just to put your good heart at rest, I will tell you one thing: the moment I choose, I can be rid of Mr. Hyde. I give you my hand upon that; and I thank you again and again; and I will just add one little word, Utterson, that I'm sure you'll take in good part: this is a private matter, and I beg of you to let it sleep."

Utterson reflected a little, looking in the fire.

"I have no doubt you are perfectly right," he said at last, getting to his feet.

"Well, but since we have touched upon this business, and for the last time, I hope," continued the doctor, "there is one point I should like you to understand. I have really a very great interest in poor Hyde. I know you have seen him; he told me so; and I fear he was rude. But I do sincerely take a great, a very great interest in that young man; and if I am taken away, Utterson, I wish you to promise me that you will bear with him and get his rights for him. I think you would, if you knew all; and it would be a weight off my mind if you would promise."

"I can't pretend that I shall ever like him," said the lawyer.

"I don't ask that," pleaded Jekyll, laying his hand upon the other's arm; "I only ask for justice; I only ask you to help him for my sake, when I am no longer here."

Utterson heaved an irrepressible sigh. "Well," said he, "I promise."

The Carew Murder Case

Nearly a year later, in the month of October, 18——, London was startled by a crime of singular ferocity, and rendered all the more notable by the high position of the victim. The details were few and startling. A maid-servant living alone in a house not far from the river had gone upstairs to bed about eleven. Although a fog rolled over the city in the small hours, the early part of the night was cloudless, and the lane, which the maid's window overlooked, was brilliantly lit by the full moon. It seems she was romantically given; for she sat down upon her box, which stood immediately under the window, and fell into a dream of musing. Never (she used to say, with streaming tears, when she narrated that experience), never had she felt more at peace with all men or thought more kindly of the world. And as she so sat she became aware of an aged and beautiful gentleman with white hair drawing near along the lane; and advancing to meet him, another and very small gentleman, to whom at first she paid less attention. When they had come within speech (which was just under the maid's eyes) the older man bowed and accosted the other with a very pretty manner of politeness. It did not seem as if the subject of his address were of great importance; indeed, from his pointing, it sometimes appeared as if he were only inquiring his way; but the moon shone on his face as he spoke, and the girl was pleased to watch it, it seemed to breathe such an innocent and old-world kindness of disposition, yet with something high too, as of a well-founded self-content. Presently her eye wandered to the other, and she was surprised to recognise in him a certain Mr. Hyde, who had once visited her master and for whom she had conceived a dislike. He had in his hand a heavy cane, with which he was trifling; but he answered never a word, and seemed to listen with an ill-contained impatience. And then all of a sudden he broke out in a great flame of anger, stamping with his foot, brandishing the cane, and carrying on (as the maid described it) like a madman. The old gentleman took a step back, with the air of one very much surprised and a trifle hurt; and at that Mr. Hyde broke out of all bounds, and clubbed him to the earth. And next moment, with ape-like fury, he was trampling his victim under foot, and hailing down a storm of blows, under which the bones were audibly shattered and the body jumped upon the roadway. At the horror of these sights and sounds, the maid fainted.

It was two o'clock when she came to herself and called for the police. The murderer was gone long ago; but there lay his victim in the middle of the lane, incredibly mangled. The stick with which the deed had been done, although it was of some rare and very tough and heavy wood, had broken in the middle under the stress of this insensate cruelty; and one splintered half had rolled in the neighbouring gutter—the other, without doubt, had been carried away by the murderer. A purse and a gold watch were found upon the victim; but, no cards or papers, except a sealed and stamped envelope, which he had been probably carrying to the post, and which bore the name and address of Mr. Utterson.

This was brought to the lawyer the next morning, before he was out of bed; and he had no sooner seen it, and been told the circumstances, than he shot out a solemn lip. "I shall say nothing till I have seen the body," said he; "this may be very serious. Have the kindness to wait while I dress." And with the same grave countenance, he hurried through his breakfast and drove to the police station, whither the body had been carried. As soon as he came into the cell, he nodded.

"Yes," said he, "I recognise him. I am sorry to say that this is Sir Danvers Carew."

"Good God, sir!" exclaimed the officer, "is it possible?" And the next moment his eye lighted up with professional ambition. "This will make a deal of noise," he said. "And perhaps you can help us to the man." And he briefly narrated what the maid had seen, and showed the broken stick.

Mr. Utterson had already quailed at the name of Hyde; but when the stick was laid before him, he could doubt no longer: broken and battered as it was, he recognised it for one that he had himself presented many years before to Henry Jekyll.

"Is this Mr. Hyde a person of small stature?" he inquired.

"Particularly small and particularly wicked-looking, is what the maid calls him," said the officer.

Mr. Utterson reflected; and then, raising his head, "If you will come with me in my cab," he said, "I think I can take you to his house."

"It was by this time about nine in the morning, and the first fog of the season. A great chocolate-coloured pall lowered over heaven, but the wind was continually charging and routing these embattled vapours; so that as the cab crawled from street to street, Mr. Utterson beheld a marvellous number of degrees and hues of twilight; for here it would be dark like the back-end of evening; and there would be a glow of a rich, lurid brown, like the light of some strange conflagration; and here, for a moment, the fog would be quite broken up, and a haggard shaft of day-light would glance in between the swirling wreaths. The dismal quarter of Soho seen under these changing glimpses, with its muddy ways, and slatternly passengers, and its lamps, which had never been extinguished or had been kindled afresh to combat this mournful reinvasion of darkness, seemed, in the lawyer's eyes, like a district of some city in a nightmare. The thoughts of his mind, besides, were of the gloomiest dye; and when he glanced at the companion of his drive, he was conscious of some touch of that terror of the law and the law's officers which may at times assail the most honest.

As the cab drew up before the address indicated, the fog lifted a little and showed him a dingy street, a gin palace, a low French eating-house, a shop for the retail of penny numbers and two-penny salads, many ragged children huddled in the doorways, and many women of many different nationalities passing out, key in hand, to have a morning glass; and the next moment the fog settled down again upon that part, as brown as umber, and cut him off from his blackguardly surroundings. This was the home of Henry Jekyll's favourite; of a man who was heir to a quarter of a million sterling.

An ivory-faced and silvery-haired old woman opened the door. She had an evil face, smoothed by hypocrisy; but her manners were excellent. Yes, she said, this was Mr. Hyde's, but he was not at home; he had been in that night very late, but had gone away again in less than an hour: there was nothing strange in that; his habits were very irregular, and he was often absent; for instance, it was nearly two months since she had seen him till yesterday.

"Very well then, we wish to see his rooms," said the lawyer; and when the woman began to declare it was impossible, "I had better tell you who this person is," he added. "This is Inspector Newcomen of Scotland Yard."

A flash of odious joy appeared upon the woman's face. "Ah!" said she, "he is in trouble! What has he done?"

Mr. Utterson and the inspector exchanged glances. "He don't seem a very popular character," observed the latter. "And now, my good woman, just let me and this gentleman have a look about us."

In the whole extent of the house, which but for the old woman remained otherwise empty, Mr. Hyde had only used a couple of rooms; but these were furnished with luxury and good taste. A closet was filled with wine; the plate was of silver, the napery elegant; a good picture hung upon the walls, a gift (as Utterson supposed) from Henry Jekyll, who was much of a connoisseur; and the carpets were of many plies and agreeable in colour. At this moment, however, the rooms bore every mark of having been recently and hurriedly ransacked; clothes lay about the floor, with their pockets inside out; lockfast drawers stood open; and on the hearth there lay a pile of grey ashes, as though many papers had been burned. From these embers the inspector disinterred the butt end of a green cheque book, which had resisted the action of the fire; the other half of the stick was found behind the door; and as this clinched his suspicions, the officer declared himself delighted. A visit to the bank, where several thousand pounds were found to be lying to the murderer's credit, completed his gratification.

"You may depend upon it, sir," he told Mr. Utterson. "I have him in my hand. He must have lost his head, or he never would have left the stick or, above all, burned the cheque book. Why, money's life to the man. We have nothing to do but wait for him at the bank, and get out the handbills."

This last, however, was not so easy of accomplishment; for Mr. Hyde had numbered few familiars—even the master of the servant-maid had only seen him twice; his family could nowhere be traced; he had never been photographed; and the few who could describe him differed widely, as common observers will. Only on one point were they agreed; and that was the haunting sense of unexpressed deformity with which the fugitive impressed his beholders.

The murder of Sir Danvers Carew, from the first illustrated edition of *Dr. Jekyll and Mr. Hyde*. (New York Public Library Picture Collection)

Incident of the Letter

It was late in the afternoon when Mr. Utterson found his way to Dr. Jekyll's door, where he was at once admitted by Poole, and carried down by the kitchen offices and across a yard which had once been a garden, to the building which was indifferently known as the laboratory or the dissecting-rooms. The doctor had bought the house from the heirs of a celebrated surgeon; and his own tastes being rather chemical than anatomical, had changed the destination of the block at the bottom of the garden. It was the first time that the lawyer had been received in that part of his friend's quarters; and he eyed the dingy windowless structure with curiosity, and gazed round with a distasteful sense of strangeness as he crossed the theatre, once crowded with eager students and now lying gaunt and silent, the tables laden with chemical apparatus, the floor strewn with crates and littered with packing straw, and the light falling dimly through the foggy cupola. At the further end, a flight of stairs mounted to a door covered with red baize; and through this Mr. Utterson was at last received into the doctor's cabinet. It was a large room, fitted round with glass presses, furnished, among other things, with a cheval-glass and a business table, and looking out upon the court by three dusty windows barred with iron. The fire burned in the grate; a lamp was set lighted on the chimney-shelf, for even in the houses the fog began to lie thickly; and there, close up to the warmth, sat Dr. Jekyll, looking deadly sick. He did not rise to meet his visitor, but held out a cold hand and bade him welcome in a changed voice.

"And now," said Mr. Utterson, as soon as Poole had left them, "you have heard the news?"

The doctor shuddered. "They were crying it in the square," he said. "I heard them in my dining room."

"One word," said the lawyer. "Carew was my client, but so are you; and I want to know what I am doing. You have not been mad enough to hide this fellow?"

"Utterson, I swear to God," cried the doctor, "I swear to God I will never set eyes on him again. I bind my honour to you that I am done with him in this world. It is all at an end. And indeed he does not want my help; you do not know him as I do; he is safe, he is quite safe; mark my words, he will never more be heard of."

The lawyer listened gloomily; he did not like his friend's feverish manner. "You seem pretty sure of him," said he; "and for your sake, I hope you may be right. If it came to a trial, your name might appear."

"I am quite sure of him," replied Jekyll; "I have grounds for certainty that I cannot share with any one. But there is one thing on which you may advise me. I have—I have received a letter; and I am at a loss whether I should show it to the police. I should like to leave it in your hands, Utterson; you would judge wisely, I am sure; I have so great a trust in you."

"You fear, I suppose, that it might lead to his detection?" asked the lawyer.

"No," said the other. "I cannot say that I care what becomes of Hyde; I am quite done with him. I was thinking of my own character, which this hateful business has rather exposed."

Utterson ruminated awhile; he was surprised at his friend's selfishness, and yet relieved by it. "Well," said he, at last, "let me see the letter."

The letter was written in an odd, upright hand, and signed "Edward Hyde": and it signified, briefly enough, that the writer's benefactor, Dr. Jekyll, whom he had long so unworthily repaid for a thousand generosities, need labour under no alarm for his safety as he had means of escape on which he placed a sure dependence. The lawyer liked this letter well enough; it put a better colour on the intimacy than he had looked for, and he blamed himself for some of his past suspicions.

"Have you the envelope?" he asked.

"I burned it," replied Jekyll, "before I thought what I was about. But it bore no postmark. The note was handed in."

"Shall I keep this and sleep upon it?," asked Utterson.

"I wish you to judge for me entirely," was the reply. "I have lost confidence in myself."

"Well, I shall consider," returned the lawyer. "And now one word more: it was Hyde who dictated the terms in your will about that disappearance?"

The doctor seemed seized with a qualm of faintness; he shut his mouth tight and nodded.

"I knew it," said Utterson. "He meant to murder you. You have had a fine escape."

"I have had what is far more to the purpose," returned the doctor solemnly: I have had a lesson—O God, Utterson, what a lesson I have had!" And he covered his face for a moment with his hands.

On his way out, the lawyer stopped and had a word or two with Poole. "By the by," said he, "there was a letter handed in today: what was the messenger like?" But Poole was positive nothing had come except by post; "and only circulars by that," he added.

This news sent off the visitor with his fears renewed. Plainly the letter had come by the laboratory door, possibly, indeed, it had been written in the cabinet; and, if that were so, it must be differently judged, and handled with the more caution. The news boys, as he went, were crying themselves hoarse along the footways: "Special edition. Shocking murder of an M.P."[1] That was the funeral oration of one friend and client; and he could not help a certain apprehension lest the good name of another should be sucked down in the eddy of the scandal. It was, at least, a ticklish decision that he had to make; and, self-reliant as he was by habit, he began to cherish a longing for advice. It was not to be had directly; but perhaps, he thought, it might be fished for.

Presently after, he sat on one side of his own hearth, with Mr. Guest, his head clerk, upon the other, and midway between,

at a nicely calculated distance from the fire, a bottle of a particular old wine that had long dwelt unsunned in the foundations of
his house. The fog still slept on the wing above the drowned city,
where the lamps glimmered like carbuncles; and through the
muffle and smother of these fallen clouds, the procession of the
town's life was still rolling in through the great arteries with a
sound as of a mighty wind. But the room was gay with firelight.
In the bottle the acids were long ago resolved; the imperial dye
had softened with time, as the colour grows richer in stained
windows; and the glow of hot autumn afternoons on hillside
vineyards was ready to be set free and to disperse the fogs of
London. Insensibly the lawyer melted. There was no man from
whom he kept fewer secrets than Mr. Guest; and he was not
always sure that he kept as many as he meant. Guest had often
been on business to the doctor's; he knew Poole; he could scarce
have failed to hear of Mr. Hyde's familiarity about the house; he
might draw conclusions: was it not as well, then, that he should
see a letter which put that mystery to rights? and above all, since
Guest, being a great student and critic of handwriting, would
consider the step natural and obliging? The clerk, besides, was a
man of counsel; he would scarce read so strange a document
without dropping a remark; and by that remark Mr. Utterson
might shape his future course.

"This is a sad business about Sir Danvers," he said.

"Yes, sir, indeed. It has elicited a great deal of public feeling,"
returned Guest. "The man, of course, was mad."

"I should like to hear your views on that," replied Utterson. "I
have a document here in his handwriting; it is between ourselves,
for I scarce know what to do about it; it is an ugly business at the
best. But there it is; quite in your way: a murderer's autograph."

Guest's eyes brightened, and he sat down at once and studied
it with passion. "No, sir," he said; "not mad; but it is an odd
hand."

"And by all accounts a very odd writer," added the lawyer.

Just then the servant entered with a note.

"Is that from Dr. Jekyll, sir?" inquired the clerk. "I thought I
knew the writing. Anything private, Mr. Utterson?"

"Only an invitation to dinner. Why? Do you want to see it?"

"One moment. I thank you, sir"; and the clerk laid the two sheets of paper alongside and sedulously compared their contents. "Thank you, sir," he said at last, returning both; "it's a very interesting autograph."

There was a pause, during which Mr. Utterson struggled with himself. "Why did you compare them, Guest?" he inquired suddenly.

"Well, sir," returned the clerk, "there's a rather singular resemblance; the two hands are in many points identical; only differently sloped."

"Rather quaint," said Utterson.

"It is, as you say, rather quaint," returned Guest.

"I wouldn't speak of this note, you know," said the master.

"No, sir," said the clerk. "I understand."

But no sooner was Mr. Utterson alone that night than he locked the note into his safe, where it reposed from that time forward. "What!" he thought. "Henry Jekyll forge for a murderer!" And his blood ran cold in his veins.

Note

1 Member of Parliament.

Remarkable Incident
of Dr. Lanyon

Time ran on; thousands of pounds were offered in reward, for the death of Sir Danvers was resented as a public injury; but Mr. Hyde had disappeared out of the ken of the police as though he had never existed. Much of his past was unearthed, indeed, and all disreputable: tales came out of the man's cruelty, at once so callous and violent, of his vile life, of his strange associates, of the hatred that seemed to have surrounded his career; but of his present whereabouts, not a whisper. From the time he had left the house in Soho on the morning of the murder, he was simply blotted out; and gradually, as time drew on, Mr. Utterson began to recover from the hotness of his alarm, and to grow more at quiet with himself. The death of Sir Danvers was, to his way of thinking, more than paid for by the disappearance of Mr. Hyde. Now that that evil influence had been withdrawn, a new life began for Dr. Jekyll. He came out of his seclusion, renewed relations with his friends, became once more their familiar guest and entertainer; and whilst he had always been known for charities, he was now no less distinguished for religion. He was busy, he was much in the open air, he did good; his face seemed to open and brighten, as if with an inward consciousness of service; and for more than two months the doctor was at peace.

On the 8th of January Utterson had dined at the doctor's with a small party; Lanyon had been there; and the face of the host had looked from one to the other as in the old days when the trio were inseparable friends. On the 12th, and again on the 14th, the door was shut against the lawyer. "The doctor was confined to the house," Poole said, "and saw no one." On the 15th he tried again, and was again refused; and having now been used for the last two months to see his friend almost daily, he found this return of solitude to weigh upon his spirits. The fifth night he had in Guest to dine with him; and the sixth he betook himself to Dr. Lanyon's.

There at least he was not denied admittance; but when he came in, he was shocked at the change which had taken place in the doctor's appearance. He had his death-warrant written legibly upon his face. The rosy man had grown pale; his flesh had fallen away; he was visibly balder and older; and yet it was not so much these tokens of a swift physical decay that arrested the lawyer's notice, as a look in the eye and quality of manner that seemed to testify to some deep-seated terror of the mind. It was unlikely that the doctor should fear death; and yet that was what Utterson was tempted to suspect. "Yes," he thought; "he is a doctor, he must know his own state and that his days are counted; and the knowledge is more than he can bear." And yet when Utterson remarked on his ill looks, it was with an air of great firmness that Lanyon declared himself a doomed man.

"I have had a shock," he said, "and I shall never recover. It is a question of weeks. Well, life has been pleasant; I liked it; yes, sir, I used to like it. I sometimes think if we knew all, we should be more glad to get away."

"Jekyll is ill, too," observed Utterson. "Have you seen him?"

But Lanyon's face changed, and he held up a trembling hand. "I wish to see or hear no more of Dr. Jekyll," he said, in a loud, unsteady voice. "I am quite done with that person; and I beg that you will spare me any allusion to one whom I regard as dead."

"Tut, tut," said Mr. Utterson; and then, after a considerable pause, "Can't I do anything?" he inquired. "We are three very old friends, Lanyon; we shall not live to make others."

"Nothing can be done," returned Lanyon; "ask himself."

"He will not see me," said the lawyer.

"I am not surprised at that," was the reply. "Some day, Utterson, after I am dead, you may perhaps come to learn the right and wrong of this. I cannot tell you. And in the meantime, if you can sit and talk with me of other things, for God's sake, stay and do so; but if you cannot keep clear of this accursed topic, then, in God's name, go, for I cannot bear it."

As soon as he got home, Utterson sat down and wrote to Jekyll, complaining of his exclusion from the house, and asking the cause of this unhappy break with Lanyon; and the next day brought him a long answer, often very pathetically worded, and sometimes darkly mysterious in drift. The quarrel with Lanyon was incurable. "I do not blame our old friend," Jekyll wrote, "but I share his view that we must never meet. I mean from henceforth to lead a life of extreme seclusion; you must not be surprised, nor must you doubt my friendship, if my door is often shut even to you. You must suffer me to go my own dark way. I have brought on myself a punishment and a danger that I cannot name. If I am the chief of sinners, I am the chief of sufferers also. I could not think that this earth contained a place for sufferings and terrors so unmanning; and you can do but one thing, Utterson, to lighten this destiny, and that is to respect my silence." Utterson was amazed; the dark influence of Hyde had been withdrawn, the doctor had returned to his old tasks and amities; a week ago, the prospect had smiled with every promise of a cheerful and an honoured age; and now in a moment, friendship and peace of mind and the whole tenor of his life were wrecked. So great and unprepared a change pointed to madness; but in view of Lanyon's manner and words, there must lie for it some deeper ground.

A week afterwards Dr. Lanyon took to his bed, and in something less than a fortnight he was dead. The night after the funeral, at which he had been sadly affected, Utterson locked the door of his business room, and sitting there by the light of a melancholy candle, drew out and set before him an envelope addressed by the hand and sealed with the seal of his dead friend. "PRIVATE: for the hands of J. G. Utterson ALONE, and in case of his predecease *to be destroyed unread*," so it was emphatically superscribed; and the lawyer dreaded to behold the contents. "I have buried one friend to-day," he thought: "what if this should cost me another?" And then he condemned the fear as a disloyalty, and broke the seal. Within there was another enclosure, likewise sealed, and marked upon the cover as "not to be opened till the death or disappearance of Dr. Henry Jekyll." Utterson could not trust his eyes. Yes, it was disappearance; here again, as in the mad will, which he had long ago restored to its author, here again were the idea of a disappearance and the name of Henry Jekyll bracketed. But in the will, that idea had sprung from the sinister suggestion of the man Hyde; it was set there with a purpose all too plain and horrible. Written by the hand of Lanyon, what should it mean? A great curiosity came to the trustee, to disregard the prohibition and dive at once to the bottom of these mysteries; but professional honour and faith to his dead friend were stringent obligations; and the packet slept in the inmost corner of his private safe.

It is one thing to mortify curiosity, another to conquer it; and it may be doubted if, from that day forth, Utterson desired the society of his surviving friend with the same eagerness. He thought of him kindly; but his thoughts were disquieted and fearful. He went to call indeed; but he was perhaps relieved to be denied admittance; perhaps, in his heart, he preferred to speak with Poole upon the doorstep, and surrounded by the air and sounds of the open city, rather than to be admitted into that house of voluntary bondage, and to sit and speak with its inscrutable recluse. Poole had, indeed, no very pleasant news to communicate. The doctor, it appeared, now more than ever confined himself to the cabinet over the laboratory, where he would sometimes even sleep; he was out of spirits, he had grown very silent, he did not read; it seemed as if he had something on his mind. Utterson became so used to the unvarying character of these reports, that he fell off little by little in the frequency of his visits.

Incident at the Window

It chanced on Sunday, when Mr. Utterson was on his usual walk with Mr. Enfield, that their way lay once again through the by street; and that when they came in front of the door, both stopped to gaze on it.

"Well," said Enfield, "that story's at an end, at least. We shall never see more of Mr. Hyde."

"I hope not," said Utterson. "Did I ever tell you that I once saw him, and shared your feeling of repulsion?"

"It was impossible to do the one without the other," returned Enfield. "And, by the way, what an ass you must have thought me, not to know that this was a back way to Dr. Jekyll's! It was partly your own fault that I found it out, even when I did."

"So you found it out, did you?" said Utterson. "But if that be so, we may step into the court and take a look at the windows. To tell you the truth, I am uneasy about poor Jekyll; and even outside, I feel as if the presence of a friend might do him good."

The court was very cool and a little damp, and full of premature twilight, although the sky, high up overhead, was still bright with sunset. The middle one of the three windows was half way open; and sitting close beside it, taking the air with an infinite sadness of mien, like some disconsolate prisoner, Utterson saw Dr. Jekyll.

"What! Jekyll!" he cried. "I trust you are better."

"I am very low, Utterson," replied the doctor drearily; "very low. It will not last long, thank God."

"You stay too much indoors," said the lawyer. "You should be out, whipping up the circulation like Mr. Enfield and me. (This is my cousin—Mr. Enfield—Dr. Jekyll.) Come, now; get your hat and take a quick turn with us."

"You are very good," sighed the other. "I should like to very much; but no, no, no, it is quite impossible; I dare not. But indeed, Utterson, I am very glad to see you; this is really a great pleasure. I would ask you and Mr. Enfield up, but the place is really not fit."

"Why then," said the lawyer, good-naturedly, "the best thing we can do is to stay down here, and speak with you from where we are."

"That is just what I was about to venture to propose," returned the doctor, with a smile. But the words were hardly uttered, before the smile was struck out of his face and succeeded by an expression of such abject terror and despair, as froze the very blood of the two gentlemen below. They saw it but for a glimpse, for the window was instantly thrust down; but that glimpse had been sufficient, and they turned and left the court without a word. In silence, too, they traversed the by street; and it was not until they had come into a neighbouring thoroughfare, where even upon a Sunday there were still some stirrings of life, that Mr. Utterson at last turned and looked at his companion. They were both pale; and there was an answering horror in their eyes.

"God forgive us! God forgive us!" said Mr. Utterson.

But Mr. Enfield only nodded his head very seriously, and walked on once more in silence.

The Last Night

M r. Utterson was sitting by his fireside one evening after dinner, when he was surprised to receive a visit from Poole.

"Bless me, Poole, what brings you here?" he cried; and then, taking a second look at him, "What ails you?" he added; "is the doctor ill?"

"Mr. Utterson," said the man, "there is something wrong."

"Take a seat, and here is a glass of wine for you," said the lawyer. "Now, take your time, and tell me plainly what you want."

"You know the doctor's ways, sir," replied Poole, "and how he shuts himself up. Well, he's shut up again in the cabinet; and I don't like it, sir—I wish I may die if I like it. Mr. Utterson, sir, I'm afraid."

"Now, my good man," said the lawyer, "be explicit. What are you afraid of?"

"I've been afraid for about a week," returned Poole, doggedly disregarding the question, "and I can bear it no more."

The man's appearance amply bore out his words; his manner was altered for the worse; and except for the moment when he had first announced his terror, he had not once looked the lawyer in the face. Even now, he sat with the glass of wine untasted on his knee, and his eyes directed to a corner of the floor. "I can bear it no more," he repeated.

"Come," said the lawyer, "I see you have some good reason, Poole; I see there is something seriously amiss. Try to tell me what it is."

"I think there's been foul play," said Poole, hoarsely.

"Foul play!" cried the lawyer, a good deal frightened, and rather inclined to be irritated in consequence. "What foul play? What does the man mean?"

"I daren't say, sir," was the answer; "but will you come along with me and see for yourself?"

Mr. Utterson's only answer was to rise and get his hat and great coat; but he observed with wonder the greatness of the relief that appeared upon the butler's face, and perhaps with no less, that the wine was still untasted when he set it down to follow.

It was a wild, cold, seasonable night of March, with a pale moon, lying on her back as though the wind had tilted her, and a flying wrack of the most diaphanous and lawny texture. The wind made talking difficult, and flecked the blood into the face. It seemed to have swept the streets unusually bare of passengers, besides; for Mr. Utterson thought he had never seen that part of London so deserted. He could have wished it otherwise; never in his life had he been conscious of so sharp a wish to see and touch his fellow-creatures; for, struggle as he might, there was borne in upon his mind a crushing anticipation of calamity. The square, when they got there, was all full of wind and dust, and the thin trees in the garden were lashing themselves along the railing. Poole, who had kept all the way a pace or two ahead, now pulled up in the middle of the pavement, and in spite of the biting weather, took off his hat and mopped his brow with a red pocket-handkerchief. But for all the hurry of his coming, these were not the dews of exertion that he wiped away, but the moisture of some strangling anguish; for his face was white, and his voice, when he spoke, harsh and broken.

"Well, sir," he said, "here we are, and God grant there be nothing wrong."

"Amen, Poole," said the lawyer.

Thereupon the servant knocked in a very guarded manner; the door was opened on the chain; and a voice asked from within, "Is that you, Poole?"

"It's all right," said Poole. "Open the door."

The hall, when they entered it, was brightly lighted up; the fire was built high; and about the hearth the whole of the servants, men and women, stood huddled together like a flock of sheep. At the sight of Mr. Utterson, the housemaid broke into hysterical whimpering; and the cook, crying out, "Bless God! it's Mr. Utterson," ran forward as if to take him in her arms.

"What, what? Are you all here?" said the lawyer, peevishly. "Very irregular, very unseemly: your master would be far from pleased."

"They're all afraid," said Poole.

Blank silence followed, no one protesting; only the maid lifted up her voice and now wept loudly.

"Hold your tongue!" Poole said to her, with a ferocity of accent that testified to his own jangled nerves; and indeed when the girl had so suddenly raised the note of her lamentation, they had all started and turned towards the inner door with faces of dreadful expectation. "And now," continued the butler, addressing the knife-boy, "reach me a candle and we'll get this through hands at once." And then he begged Mr. Utterson to follow him, and led the way to the back garden.

"Now, sir," said he, "you come as gently as you can. I want you to hear, and I don't want you to be heard. And see here, sir, if by any chance he was to ask you in, don't go."

Mr. Utterson's nerves, at this unlooked-for termination, gave a jerk that nearly threw him from his balance; but he recollected his courage, and followed the butler into the laboratory building and through the surgical theatre, with its lumber of crates and bottles, to the foot of the stair. Here Poole motioned him to stand on one side and listen; while he himself, setting down the candle and making a great and obvious call on his resolution, mounted the steps, and knocked with a somewhat uncertain hand on the red baize of the cabinet door.

"Mr. Utterson, sir, asking to see you," he called; and even as he did so, once more violently signed to the lawyer to give ear.

A voice answered from within: "Tell him I cannot see any one," it said, complainingly.

"Thank you, sir," said Poole, with a note of something like triumph in his voice; and taking up his candle, he led Mr. Utterson back across the yard and into the great kitchen, where the fire was out and the beetles were leaping on the floor.

"Sir," he said, looking Mr. Utterson in the eyes, "was that my master's voice?"

"It seems much changed," replied the lawyer, very pale, but giving look for look.

"Changed? Well, yes, I think so," said the butler. "Have I been twenty years in this man's house, to be deceived about his voice? No, sir; master's made away with; he was made away with eight days ago, when we heard him cry out upon the name of God; and *who's* in there instead of him, and *why* it stays there, is a thing that cries to Heaven, Mr. Utterson!"

"This is a very strange tale, Poole; this is rather a wild tale, my man," said Mr. Utterson, biting his finger. "Suppose it were as you suppose, supposing, Dr. Jekyll to have been—well, murdered, what could induce the murderer to stay? That won't hold water; it doesn't commend itself to reason."

"Well, Mr. Utterson, you are a hard man to satisfy, but I'll do it yet," said Poole. "All this last week (you must know) him, or it, or whatever it is that lives in that cabinet, has been crying night and day for some sort of medicine and cannot get it to his mind. It was sometimes his way—the master's, that is—to write his orders on a sheet of paper and throw it on the stair. We've had nothing else this week back; nothing but papers, and a closed door, and the very meals left there to be smuggled in when nobody was looking. Well, sir, every day, ay, and twice and thrice in the same day, there have been orders and complaints, and I have been sent flying to all the wholesale chemists in town. Every time I brought the stuff back, there would be another paper telling me to return it, because it was not pure, and another order to a different firm. This drug is wanted bitter bad, sir, whatever for."

"Have you any of these papers?" asked Mr. Utterson.

Poole felt in his pocket and handed out a crumpled note, which the lawyer, bending nearer to the candle, carefully examined. Its contents ran thus: "Dr. Jekyll presents his compliments to Messrs. Maw. He assures them that their last sample is impure and quite useless for his present purpose. In the year 18——, Dr. J. purchased a somewhat large quantity from Messrs. M. He now begs them to search with the most sedulous care, and should any of the same quality be left, to forward it to him at once. Expense is no consideration. The importance of this to Dr. J. can hardly be exaggerated." So far the letter had run composedly enough; but here, with a sudden splutter of the pen, the writer's emotion had broken loose. "For God's sake," he had added, "find me some of the old."

"This is a strange note," said Mr. Utterson; and then sharply, "How do you come to have it open?"

"The man at Maw's was main angry, sir, and he threw it back to me like so much dirt," returned Poole.

"This is unquestionably the doctor's hand, do you know?" resumed the lawyer.

"I thought it looked like it," said the servant, rather sulkily; and then, with another voice, "But what matters hand of write?" he said. "I've seen him!"

"Seen him?" repeated Mr. Utterson. "Well?"

"That's it!" said Poole. "It was this way. I came suddenly into the theatre from the garden. It seems he had slipped out to look for this drug, or whatever it is; for the cabinet door was open, and there he was at the far end of the room digging among the crates. He looked up when I came in, gave a kind of cry, and whipped upstairs into the cabinet. It was but for one minute that I saw him, but the hair stood upon my head like quills. Sir, if that was my master, why had he a mask upon his face? If it was my master, why did he cry out like a rat and run from me? I have served him long enough. And then . . ." the man paused and passed his hand over his face.

"These are all very strange circumstances," said Mr. Utterson, "but I think I begin to see daylight. Your master, Poole, is plainly seized with one of those maladies that both torture and deform the sufferer; hence, for aught I know, the alteration of his voice; hence the mask and his avoidance of his friends; hence his eagerness to find this drug, by means of which the poor soul retains some hope of ultimate recovery—God grant that he be not deceived! There is my explanation; it is sad enough, Poole, ay, and appalling to consider; but it is plain and natural, hangs well together and delivers us from all exorbitant alarms."

"Sir," said the butler, turning to a sort of mottled pallor, "that thing was not my master, and there's the truth. My master"— here he looked round him, and began to whisper—"is a tall fine build of a man, and this was more of a dwarf." Utterson attempted to protest. "O, sir," cried Poole, "do you think I do not know my master after twenty years? do you think I do not know where his head comes to in the cabinet door, where I saw him every morning of my life? No, sir, that thing in the mask was never Dr. Jekyll—God knows what it was, but it was never Dr. Jekyll; and it is the belief of my heart that there was murder done."

"Poole," replied the lawyer, "if you say that, it will become my duty to make certain. Much as I desire to spare your master's feelings, much as I am puzzled about this note, which seems to prove him to be still alive, I shall consider it my duty to break in that door."

"Ah, Mr. Utterson, that's talking!" cried the butler.

"And now comes the second question," resumed Utterson: "Who is going to do it?"

"Why, you and me, sir," was the undaunted reply.

"That is very well said," returned the lawyer; "and whatever comes of it, I shall make it my business to see you are no loser."

"There is an axe in the theatre," continued Poole; "and you might take the kitchen poker for yourself."

The lawyer took that rude but weighty instrument into his hand, and balanced it. "Do you know, Poole," he said, looking up, "that you and I are about to place ourselves in a position of some peril?"

"You may say so, sir, indeed," returned the butler.

"It is well, then, that we should be frank," said the other. "We both think more than we have said; let us make a clean breast. This masked figure that you saw, did you recognise it?"

"Well, sir, it went so quick, and the creature was so doubled up, that I could hardly swear to that," was the answer. "But if you mean, was it Mr. Hyde?—why, yes, I think it was! You see, it was much of the same bigness; and it had the same quick light way with it; and then who else could have got in by the laboratory door? You have not forgot, sir, that at the time of the murder he had still the key with him? But, that's not all. I don't know, Mr. Utterson, if ever you met this Mr. Hyde?"

"Yes," said the lawyer, "I once spoke with him."

"Then you must know, as well as the rest of us, that there was something queer about that gentleman—something that gave a man a turn—I don't know rightly how to say it, sir, beyond this: that you felt in your marrow—kind of cold and thin."

"I own I felt something of what you describe," said Mr. Utterson.

"Quite so, sir," returned Poole. "Well, when that masked thing like a monkey jumped up from among the chemicals and whipped into the cabinet, it went down my spine like ice. O, I know it's not evidence, Mr. Utterson; I'm book-learned enough for that; but a man has his feelings; and I give you my bible-word it was Mr. Hyde!"

"Ay, ay," said the lawyer. "My fears incline to the same point. Evil, I fear, founded—evil was sure to come—of that connection. Ay, truly, I believe you; I believe poor Harry is killed; and I believe his murderer (for what purpose, God alone can tell) is still lurking in his victim's room. Well, let our name be vengeance. Call Bradshaw."

The footman came at the summons, very white and nervous.

"Pull yourself together, Bradshaw," said the lawyer. "This suspense, I know, is telling upon all of you; but it is now our intention to make an end of it. Poole, here, and I are going to force our way into the cabinet. If all is well, my shoulders are broad enough to bear the blame. Meanwhile, lest anything should really be amiss, or any malefactor seek to escape by the back, you and the boy must go round the corner with a pair of good sticks, and take your post at the laboratory door. We give you ten minutes, to get to your stations."

As Bradshaw left, the lawyer looked at his watch. "And now, Poole, let us get to ours," he said; and taking the poker under his arm, he led the way into the yard. The scud had banked over the moon, and it was now quite dark. The wind, which only broke in puffs and draughts into that deep well of building, tossed the light of the candle to and fro about their steps, until they came into the shelter of the theatre, where they sat down silently to wait. London hummed solemnly all around; but nearer at hand, the stillness was only broken by the sound of a footfall moving to and fro along the cabinet floor.

"So it will walk all day, sir," whispered Poole; "ay, and the better part of the night. Only when a new sample comes from the chemist, there's a bit of a break. Ah, it's an ill conscience that's such an enemy to rest! Ah, sir, there's blood foully shed in every step of it! But hark again, a little closer—put your heart in your ears Mr. Utterson, and tell me, is that the doctor's foot?"

The steps fell lightly and oddly, with a certain swing, for all they went so slowly; it was different indeed from the heavy creaking tread of Henry Jekyll. Utterson sighed. "Is there never anything else?" he asked.

Poole nodded. "Once," he said. "Once I heard it weeping!"

"Weeping? how that?" said the lawyer, conscious of a sudden chill of horror.

"Weeping like a woman or a lost soul," said the butler. "I came away with that upon my heart, that I could have wept too."

But now the ten minutes drew to an end. Poole disinterred the axe from under a stack of packing straw; the candle was set upon the nearest table to light them to the attack; and they drew near with bated breath to where the patient foot was still going up and down, up and down in the quiet of the night.

"Jekyll," cried Utterson, with a loud voice, "I demand to see you." He paused a moment, but there came no reply. "I give you fair warning, our suspicions are aroused, and I must and shall see you," he resumed; "if not by fair means, then by foul—if not of your consent, then by brute force!"

"Utterson," said the voice, "for God's sake, have mercy!"

"Ah, that's not Jekyll's voice—it's Hyde's!" cried Utterson. "Down with the door, Poole!"

Poole swung the axe over his shoulder; the blow shook the building, and the red baize door leaped against the lock and hinges. A dismal screech, as of mere animal terror, rang from the cabinet. Up went the axe again, and again the panels crashed and the frame bounded; four times the blow fell; but the wood was tough and the fittings were of excellent workmanship; and it was not until the fifth that the lock burst in sunder, and the wreck of the door fell inwards on the carpet.

The besiegers, appalled by their own riot and the stillness that had succeeded, stood back a little and peered in. There lay the cabinet before their eyes in the quiet lamplight, a good fire glowing and chattering on the hearth, the kettle singing its thin strain, a drawer or two open, papers neatly set forth on the business table, and nearer the fire, the things laid out for tea; the quietest room, you would have said, and, but for the glazed presses full of chemicals, the most commonplace that night in London.

Right in the midst there lay the body of a man sorely contorted and still twitching. They drew near on tiptoe, turned it on its back, and beheld the face of Edward Hyde. He was dressed in clothes far too large for him, clothes of the doctor's bigness; the cords of his face still moved with a semblance of life, but life was quite gone; and by the crushed phial in the hand and the strong smell of kernels that hung upon the air, Utterson knew that he was looking on the body of a self-destroyer.

"We have come too late," he said sternly, "whether to save or punish. Hyde is gone to his account; and it only remains for us to find the body of your master."

The far greater proportion of the building was occupied by the theatre, which filled almost the whole ground storey, and was lighted from above, and by the cabinet, which formed an upper storey at one end and looked upon the court. A corridor joined the theatre to the door on the by street; and with this, the cabinet communicated separately by a second flight of stairs. There were besides a few dark closets and a spacious cellar. All these they now thoroughly examined. Each closet needed but a glance, for all they were empty and all, by the dust that fell from their doors, had stood long unopened. The cellar, indeed, was filled with crazy lumber, mostly dating from the times of the surgeon who was Jekyll's predecessor; but even as they opened the door, they were advertised of the uselessness of further search by the fall of a perfect mat of cobweb which had for years sealed up the entrance. Nowhere was there any trace of Henry Jekyll, dead or alive.

Poole stamped on the flags of the corridor. "He must be buried here," he said, hearkening to the sound.

"Or he may have fled," said Utterson, and he turned to examine the door in the by street. It was locked; and lying near by on the flags, they found the key, already stained with rust.

"This does not look like use," observed the lawyer.

"Use!" echoed Poole. "Do you not see, sir, it is broken? much as if a man had stamped on it."

"Ah," continued Utterson, "and the fractures, too, are rusty." The two men looked at each other with a scare. "This is beyond me, Poole," said the lawyer. "Let us go back to the cabinet."

They mounted the stair in silence, and still, with an occasional awestruck glance at the dead body, proceeded more thoroughly to examine the contents of the cabinet. At one table, there were traces of chemical work, various measured heaps of some white salt being laid on glass saucers, as though for an experiment in which the unhappy man had been prevented.

"That is the same drug that I was always bringing him," said Poole; and even as he spoke, the kettle with a startling noise boiled over.

This brought them to the fireside, where the easy chair was drawn cosily up, and the tea things stood ready to the sitter's elbow, the very sugar in the cup. There were several books on a shelf; one lay beside the tea things open, and Utterson was amazed to find it a copy of a pious work for which Jekyll had several times expressed a great esteem, annotated, in his own hand, with startling blasphemies.

Next, in the course of their review of the chamber, the searchers came to the cheval-glass, into whose depth they looked with an involuntary horror. But it was so turned as to show them nothing but the rosy glow playing on the roof, the fire sparkling in a hundred repetitions along the glazed front of the presses, and their own pale and fearful countenances stooping to look in.

"This glass has seen some strange things, sir," whispered Poole.

"And surely none stranger than itself," echoed the lawyer, in the same tone. "For what did Jekyll"—he caught himself up at the word with a start, and then conquering the weakness: "what could Jekyll want with it?" he said.

"You may say that!" said Poole.

Next they turned to the business table. On the desk, among the neat array of papers, a large envelope was uppermost, and bore, in the doctor's hand, the name of Mr. Utterson. The lawyer unsealed it, and several enclosures fell to the floor. The first was a will, drawn in the same eccentric terms as the one which he had returned six months before, to serve as a testament in case of death and as a deed of gift in case of disappearance; but in place of the name of Edward Hyde, the lawyer, with indescribable amazement, read the name of Gabriel John Utterson. He looked at Poole, and then back at the papers, and last of all at the dead malefactor stretched upon the carpet.

"My head goes round," he said. "He has been all these days in possession; he had no cause to like me; he must have raged to see himself displaced; and he has not destroyed this document."

He caught the next paper; it was a brief note in the doctor's hand and dated at the top. "O Poole!" the lawyer cried, "he was alive and here this day. He cannot have been disposed of in so short a space; he must be still alive, he must have fled! And then, why fled? and how? and in that case can we venture to declare this suicide? O, we must be careful. I foresee that we may yet involve your master in some dire catastrophe."

"Why don't you read it, sir?" asked Poole.

"Because I fear," replied the lawyer, solemnly. "God grant I have no cause for it!" And with that he brought the paper to his eyes, and read as follows:

> My dear Utterson,—When this shall fall into your hands, I shall have disappeared, under what circumstances I have not the penetration to foresee, but my instinct and all the circumstances of my nameless situation tell me that the end is sure and must be early. Go then, and first read the narrative which Lanyon warned me he was to place in your hands; and if you care to hear more, turn to the confession of
>
> Your unworthy and unhappy friend,
>
> Henry Jekyll

"There was a third enclosure," asked Utterson.

"Here, sir," said Poole, and gave into his hands a considerable packet sealed in several places.

The lawyer put it in his pocket. "I would say nothing of this paper. If your master has fled or is dead, we may at least save his credit. It is now ten; I must go home and read these documents in quiet; but I shall be back before midnight, when we shall send for the police."

They went out, locking the door of the theatre behind them; and Utterson, once more leaving the servants gathered about the fire in the hall, trudged back to his office to read the two narratives in which this mystery was now to be explained.

Dr. Lanyon's Narrative

On the ninth of January, now four days ago, I received by the evening delivery a registered envelope, addressed in the hand of my colleague and old school-companion, Henry Jekyll. I was a good deal surprised by this; for we were by no means in the habit of correspondence; I had seen the man, dined with him, indeed, the night before; and I could imagine nothing in our intercourse that should justify the formality of registration. The contents increased my wonder; for this is how the letter ran:

10th December 18——

DEAR LANYON,—You are one of my oldest friends; and although we may have differed at times on scientific questions, I cannot remember, at least on my side, any break in our affection. There was never a day when, if you had said to me, "Jekyll, my life, my honour, my reason, depend upon you," I would not have sacrificed my fortune or my left hand to help you. Lanyon, my life, my honour, my reason, are all at your mercy; if you fail me to-night, I am lost. You might suppose, after this preface, that I am going to ask you for something dishonourable to grant. Judge for yourself.

I want you to postpone all other engagements for to-night—ay, even if you were summoned to the bedside of an emperor; to take a cab, unless your carriage should be actually at the door; and, with this letter in your hand for consultation, to drive straight to my house. Poole, my butler, has his orders; you will find him waiting your arrival with a locksmith. The door of my cabinet is then to be forced; and you are to go in alone; to open the glazed press (letter E) on the left hand, breaking the lock if it be shut; and to draw out, *with all its contents as they stand*, the fourth drawer from the top or (which is the same thing) the third from the bottom. In my extreme distress of mind, I have a morbid fear of misdirecting you; but even if I am in error, you may know the right drawer by its contents: some powders, a phial, and a paper book. This drawer I beg of you to carry back with you to Cavendish Square exactly as it stands.

That is the first part of the service: now for the second. You should be back, if you set out at once on the receipt of this, long before midnight; but I will leave you that amount of margin, not only in the fear of one of those obstacles that can neither be prevented nor foreseen, but because an hour when your servants are in bed is to be preferred for what will then remain to do. At midnight, then, I have to ask you to be alone in your consulting-room, to admit with your own hand into the house a man who will present himself in my name, and to place in his hands the drawer that you will have brought with you from my cabinet. Then you will have played your part and earned my gratitude completely. Five minutes afterwards, if you insist upon an explanation, you will have understood that these arrangements are of capital importance; and that by the neglect of one of them, fantastic as they must appear, you might have charged your conscience with my death or the shipwreck of my reason.

Confident as I am that you will not trifle with this appeal, my heart sinks and my hand trembles at the bare thought of such a possibility. Think of me at this hour, in a strange place, labouring under a blackness of distress that no fancy can exaggerate, and yet well aware that, if you will but punctually serve me, my troubles will roll away like a story that is told. Serve me, my dear Lanyon, and save

Your friend,

H.J.

PS.—I had already sealed this up when a fresh terror struck upon my soul. It is possible that the post office may fail me, and this letter not come into your hands until to-morrow morning. In that case, dear Lanyon, do my errand when it shall be most convenient for you in the course of the day; and once more expect my messenger at midnight. It may then already be too late; and if that night passes without event, you will know that you have seen the last of Henry Jekyll.

Upon the reading of this letter, I made sure my colleague was insane; but till that was proved beyond the possibility of doubt, I felt bound to do as he requested. The less I understood of this farrago, the less I was in a position to judge of its importance; and an appeal so worded could not be set aside without a grave responsibility. I rose accordingly from table, got into a hansom, and drove straight to Jekyll's house. The butler was awaiting my arrival; he had received by the same post as mine a registered letter of instruction, and had sent at once for a locksmith and a carpenter. The tradesmen came while we were yet speaking; and we moved in a body to old Dr. Denman's surgical theatre, from which (as you are doubtless aware) Jekyll's private cabinet is most conveniently entered. The door was very strong, the lock excellent; the carpenter avowed he would have great trouble, and have to do much damage, if force were to be used; and the locksmith was near despair. But this last was a handy fellow, and after two hours' work, the door stood open. The press marked E was unlocked; and I took out the drawer, had it filled up with straw and tied in a sheet, and returned with it to Cavendish Square.

Here I proceeded to examine its contents. The powders were neatly enough made up, but not with the nicety of the dispensing chemist; so that it was plain they were of Jekyll's private manufacture; and when I opened one of the wrappers, I found what seemed to me a simple crystalline salt of a white colour. The phial, to which I next turned my attention, might have been about half-full of a blood-red liquor, which was highly pungent to the sense of smell, and seemed to me to contain phosphorus and some volatile ether. At the other ingredients I could make no guess. The book was an ordinary version book, and contained little but a series of dates. These covered a period of many years, but I observed that the entries ceased nearly a year ago and quite abruptly. Here and there a brief remark was appended to a date, usually no more than a single word: "double" occurring perhaps six times in a total of several hundred entries; and once very early in the list and followed by several marks of exclamation, "total failure!!!" All this, though it whetted my curiosity, told me little that was definite. Here were a phial of some tincture, a paper of some salt, and the record of a series of experiments that had led (like too many of Jekyll's investigations) to no end of practical usefulness. How could the presence of these articles in my house

affect either the honour, the sanity, or the life of my flighty colleague? If his messenger could go to one place, why could he not
go to another? And even granting some impediment, why was
this gentleman to be received by me in secret? The more I
reflected, the more convinced I grew that I was dealing with a
case of cerebral disease; and though I dismissed my servants to bed,
I loaded an old revolver, that I might be found in some posture of
self-defence.

Twelve o'clock had scarce rung out over London, ere the
knocker sounded very gently on the door. I went myself at the
summons, and found a small man crouching against the pillars
of the portico.

"Are you come from Dr. Jekyll?" I asked.

He told me "yes" by a constrained gesture; and when I had
bidden him enter, he did not obey me without a searching backward glance into the darkness of the square. There was a policeman not far off, advancing with his bull's eye open; and at the
sight, I thought my visitor started and made greater haste.

These particulars struck me, I confess, disagreeably; and as I
followed him into the bright light of the consulting-room, I kept
my hand ready on my weapon. Here, at last, I had a chance of
clearly seeing him. I had never set eyes on him before, so much
was certain. He was small, as I have said; I was struck besides
with the shocking expression of his face, with his remarkable
combination of great muscular activity and great apparent debility
of constitution, and—last but not least—with the odd, subjective
disturbance caused by his neighbourhood. This bore some
resemblance to incipient rigor, and was accompanied by a
marked sinking of the pulse. At the time, I set it down to some
idiosyncratic, personal distaste, and merely wondered at the
acuteness of the symptoms; but I have since had reason to believe
the cause to lie much deeper in the nature of man, and to turn on
some nobler hinge than the principle of hatred.

This person (who had thus, from the first moment of his
entrance, struck in me what I can only describe as a disgustful
curiosity) was dressed in a fashion that would have made an
ordinary person laughable; his clothes, that is to say, although
they were of rich and sober fabric, were enormously too large for

him in every measurement—the trousers hanging on his legs and rolled up to keep them from the ground, the waist of the coat below his haunches, and the collar sprawling wide upon his shoulders. Strange to relate, this ludicrous accoutrement was far from moving me to laughter. Rather, as there was something abnormal and misbegotten in the very essence of the creature that now faced me—something seizing, surprising and revolting—this fresh disparity seemed but to fit in with and to reinforce it; so that to my interest in the man's nature and character there was added a curiosity as to his origin, his life, his fortune and status in the world.

These observations, though they have taken so great a space to be set down in, were yet the work of a few seconds. My visitor was, indeed, on fire with sombre excitement.

"Have you got it?" he cried. "Have you got it?" And so lively was his impatience that he even laid his hand upon my arm and sought to shake me.

I put him back conscious at his touch of a certain icy pang along my blood. "Come, sir," said I. "You forget that I have not yet the pleasure of your acquaintance. Be seated, if you please." And I showed him an example, and sat down myself in my customary seat and with as fair an imitation of my ordinary manner to a patient, as the lateness of the hour, the nature of my pre-occupations, and the horror I had of my visitor would suffer me to muster.

"I beg your pardon, Dr. Lanyon," he replied, civilly enough. "What you say is very well founded; and my impatience has shown its heels to my politeness. I come here at the instance of your colleague, Dr. Henry Jekyll, on a piece of business of some moment; and I understood . . ." he paused and put his hand to his throat, and I could see, in spite of his collected manner, that he was wrestling against the approaches of the hysteria—"I understood, a drawer . . ."

But here I took pity on my visitor's suspense, and some perhaps on my own growing curiosity.

"There it is, sir," said I, pointing to the drawer where it lay on the floor behind a table, and still covered with the sheet.

He sprang to it, and then paused, and laid his hand upon his heart; I could hear his teeth grate with the convulsive action of his jaws; and his face was so ghastly to see that I grew alarmed both for his life and reason.

"Compose yourself," said I.

He turned a dreadful smile to me, and, as if with the decision of despair, plucked away the sheet. At sight of the contents, he uttered one loud sob of such immense relief that I sat petrified. And the next moment, in a voice that was already fairly well under control, "Have you a graduated glass?" he asked.

I rose from my place with something of an effort, and gave him what he asked.

He thanked me with a smiling nod, measured but a few minims of the red tincture and added one of the powders. The mixture, which was at first of a reddish hue, began, in proportion as the crystals melted, to brighten in colour, to effervesce audibly, and to throw off small fumes of vapour. Suddenly, and at the same moment, the ebullition ceased, and the compound changed to a dark purple, which faded again more slowly to a watery green. My visitor, who had watched these metamorphoses with a keen eye, smiled, set down the glass upon the table, and then turned and looked upon me with an air of scrutiny.

"And now," said he, "to settle what remains. Will you be wise? will you be guided? will you suffer me to take this glass in my hand, and to go forth from your house without further parley? or has the greed of curiosity too much command of you? Think before you answer, for it shall be done as you decide. As you decide, you shall be left as you were before, and neither richer nor wiser, unless the sense of service rendered to a man in mortal distress may be counted as a kind of riches of the soul. Or, if you shall so prefer to choose, a new province of knowledge and new avenues to fame and power shall be laid open to you, here, in this room, upon the instant; and your sight shall be blasted by a prodigy to stagger the unbelief of Satan."

"Sir," said I, affecting a coolness that I was far from truly possessing, "you speak enigmas, and you will perhaps not wonder that I hear you with no very strong impression of belief. But I have gone too far in the way of inexplicable services to pause before I see the end."

"It is well," replied my visitor. "Lanyon, you remember your vows: what follows is under the seal of our profession. And now, you who have so long been bound to the most narrow and material views, you who have denied the virtue of transcendental medicine, you who have derided your superiors—behold!"

He put the glass to his lips, and drank at one gulp. A cry followed; he reeled, staggered, clutched at the table and held on, staring with injected eyes, gasping with open mouth; and as I looked, there came, I thought, a change—he seemed to swell—his face became suddenly black, and the features seemed to melt and alter—and the next moment I had sprung to my feet and leaped back against the wall, my arm raised to shield me from that prodigy, my mind submerged in terror.

"O God!" I screamed, and "O God!" again and again; for there before my eyes—pale and shaken, and half fainting, and groping before him with his hands, like a man restored from death—there stood Henry Jekyll!

What he told me in the next hour I cannot bring my mind to set on paper. I saw what I saw, I heard what I heard, and my soul sickened at it; and yet, now when that sight has faded from my eyes, I ask myself if I believe it, and I cannot answer. My life is shaken to its roots; sleep has left me; the deadliest terror sits by me at all hours of the day and night; I feel that my days are numbered, and that I must die; and yet I shall die incredulous. As for the moral turpitude that man unveiled to me, even with tears of penitence, I cannot, even in memory, dwell on it without a start of horror. I will say but one thing, Utterson, and that (if you can bring your mind to credit it) will be more than enough. The creature who crept into my house that night was, on Jekyll's own confession, known by the name of Hyde and hunted for in every corner of the land as the murderer of Carew.

HASTIE LANYON

Henry Jekyll's Full Statement of the Case

I was born in the year 18—— to a large fortune, endowed besides with excellent parts, inclined by nature to industry, fond of the respect of the wise and good among my fellow-men, and thus, as might have been supposed, with every guarantee of an honourable and distinguished future. And indeed, the worst of my faults was a certain impatient gaiety of disposition, such as has made the happiness of many, but such as I found it hard to reconcile with my imperious desire to carry my head high, and wear a more than commonly grave countenance before the public. Hence it came about that I concealed my pleasures; and that when I reached years of reflection, and began to look round me and take stock of my progress and position in the world, I stood already committed to a profound duplicity of life. Many a man would have even blazoned such irregularities as I was guilty of; but from the high views that I had set before me, I regarded and hid them with an almost morbid sense of shame. It was thus rather the exacting nature of my aspirations, than any particular degradation in my faults, that made me what I was and, with even a deeper trench than in the majority of men, severed in me those provinces of good and ill which divide and compound man's dual nature. In this case, I was driven to reflect deeply and inveterately on that hard law of life which lies at the root of religion, and is one of the most plentiful springs of distress. Though so profound a double-dealer, I was in no sense a hypocrite; both sides of me were in dead earnest; I was no more myself when I laid aside restraint and plunged in shame, than when I laboured, in the eye of day, at the furtherance of knowledge or the relief of sorrow and suffering. And it chanced that the direction of my scientific studies, which led wholly towards the mystic and the transcendental, reacted and shed a strong light on this consciousness of the perennial war among my members. With every day, and from both sides of my intelligence, the moral and the intellectual, I thus drew steadily nearer to that truth by whose partial discovery I have been doomed to such a dreadful shipwreck: that man, is not truly one, but truly two. I say two, because the state of my own knowledge does not pass beyond that point. Others will follow, others will outstrip me on the same lines; and I hazard the guess that man will be ultimately known for a mere polity of multifarious, incongruous and independent denizens. I, for my part, from the nature of my life, advanced infallibly in one direction and in one direction only. It was on the moral side, and in my own person, that I learned to recognise the thorough and primitive duality of man; I saw that, of the two natures that contended in the field of my consciousness, even if I could rightly be said to be either, it was only because I was radically both; and from an early date, even before the course of my scientific discoveries had begun to suggest the most naked possibility of such a miracle, I had learned to dwell with pleasure, as a beloved daydream, on the thought of the separation of these elements. If each, I told myself, could but be housed in separate identities, life would be relieved of all that was unbearable; the unjust might go his way, delivered from the aspirations and remorse of his more upright twin; and the just could walk steadfastly and securely on his upward path, doing the good things in which he found his pleasure, and no longer exposed to disgrace and penitence by the hands of this extraneous evil. It was the curse of mankind that these incongruous faggots were thus bound together—that in the agonised womb of consciousness these polar twins should be continuously struggling. How, then, were they dissociated?

I was so far in my reflections when, as I have said, a side light began to shine upon the subject from the laboratory table. I began to perceive more deeply than it has ever yet been stated, the trembling immateriality, the mist-like transience, of this seemingly so solid body in which we walk attired. Certain agents I found to have the power to shake and to pluck back that fleshly vestment, even as a wind might toss the curtains of a pavilion. For two good reasons, I will not enter deeply into this scientific branch of my confession. First, because I have been made to learn that the doom and burthen of our life is bound for ever on man's shoulders; and when the attempt is made to cast it off, it but returns upon us with more unfamiliar and more awful pressure. Second, because, as my narrative will make, alas! too evident, my discoveries were incomplete. Enough, then, that I not only recognised my natural body for the mere aura and effulgence of certain of the powers that made up my spirit, but managed to compound a drug by which these powers should be dethroned from their supremacy, and a second form and countenance substituted, none the less natural to me because they were the expression, and bore the stamp, of lower elements in my soul.

I hesitated long before I put this theory to the test of practice. I knew well that I risked death; for any drug that so potently controlled and shook the very fortress of identity, might by the least scruple of an overdose or at the least inopportunity in the moment of exhibition, utterly blot out that immaterial tabernacle which I looked to it to change. But the temptation of a discovery so singular and profound at last overcame the suggestions of alarm. I had long since prepared my tincture; I purchased at once, from a firm of wholesale chemists, a large quantity of a particular salt, which I knew, from my experiments, to be the last ingredient required; and, late one accursed night I compounded the elements, watched them boil and smoke together in the glass, and when the ebullition had subsided, with a strong glow of courage, drank off the potion.

The most racking pangs succeeded: a grinding in the bones, deadly nausea, and a horror of the spirit that cannot be exceeded at the hour of birth or death. Then these agonies began swiftly to subside, and I came to myself as if out of a great sickness. There was something strange in my sensations, something indescribably new and, from its very novelty, incredibly sweet. I felt younger, lighter, happier in body; within I was conscious of a heady recklessness, a current of disordered sensual images running like a mill race in my fancy, a solution of the bonds of obligation, an unknown but not an innocent freedom of the soul. I knew myself, at the first breath of this new life, to be more wicked, tenfold more wicked, sold a slave to my original evil; and the thought, in that moment, braced and delighted me like wine. I stretched out my hands, exulting in the freshness of these sensations; and in the act, I was suddenly aware that I had lost in stature.

There was no mirror, at that date, in my room; that which stands beside me as I write was brought there later on, and for the very purpose of those transformations. The night, however, was far gone into the morning—the morning, black as it was, was nearly ripe for the conception of the day—the inmates of my house were locked in the most rigorous hours of slumber; and I determined, flushed as I was with hope and triumph, to venture in my new shape as far as to my bedroom. I crossed the yard, wherein the constellations looked down upon me, I could have thought, with wonder, the first creature of that sort that their unsleeping vigilance had yet disclosed to them; I stole through the corridors, a stranger in my own house; and coming to my room, I saw for the first time the appearance of Edward Hyde.

I must here speak by theory alone, saying not that which I know, but that which I suppose to be most probable. The evil side of my nature, to which I had now transferred the stamping efficacy, was less robust and less developed than the good which I had just deposed. Again, in the course of my life, which had been, after all, nine-tenths a life of effort, virtue and control, it had been much less exercised and much less exhausted. And hence, as I think, it came about that Edward Hyde was so much smaller, slighter, and younger than Henry Jekyll. Even as good shone upon the countenance of the one, evil was written broadly and plainly on the face of the other. Evil besides (which I must still believe to be the lethal side of man) had left on that body an imprint of deformity and decay. And yet when I looked upon that ugly idol in the glass, I was conscious of no repugnance, rather of a leap of welcome. This, too, was myself. It seemed natural and human. In my eyes it bore a livelier image of the spirit, it seemed more express and single, than the imperfect and divided countenance, I had been hitherto accustomed to call mine. And in so far I was doubtless right. I have observed that when I wore the semblance of Edward Hyde, none could come near to me at first without a visible misgiving of the flesh. This, as I take it, was because all human beings, as we meet them, are commingled out of good and evil: and Edward Hyde, alone, in the ranks of mankind, was pure evil.

I lingered but a moment at the mirror: the second and conclusive experiment had yet to be attempted; it yet remained to be seen if I had lost my identity beyond redemption and must flee before daylight from a house that was no longer mine; and hurrying back to my cabinet, I once more prepared and drank the cup, once more suffered the pangs of dissolution, and came to myself once more with the character, the stature, and the face of Henry Jekyll.

That night I had come to the fatal cross roads. Had I approached my discovery in a more noble spirit, had I risked the experiment while under the empire of generous or pious aspirations, all must have been otherwise, and from these agonies of death and birth I had come forth an angel instead of a fiend. The drug had no discriminating action; it was neither diabolical nor divine; it but shook the doors of the prisonhouse of my disposition; and, like the captives of Philippi,[1] that which stood within ran forth. At that time my virtue slumbered; my evil, kept awake by ambition, was alert and swift to seize the occasion; and the thing that was projected was Edward Hyde. Hence, although I had now two characters as well as two appearances, one was wholly evil, and the other was still the old Henry Jekyll, that incongruous compound of whose reformation and improvement I had already learned to despair. The movement was thus wholly toward the worse.

Even at that time, I had not yet conquered my aversion to the dryness of a life of study. I would still be merrily disposed at times; and as my pleasures were (to say the least) undignified, and I was not only well known and highly considered, but growing towards the elderly man, this incoherency of my life was daily growing more unwelcome. It was on this side that my new power tempted me until I fell in slavery. I had but to drink the cup, to doff at once the body of the noted professor, and to assume, like a thick cloak, that of Edward Hyde. I smiled at the notion; it seemed to me at the time to be humorous; and I made my preparations with the most studious care. I took and furnished that house in Soho to which Hyde was tracked by the police; and engaged as housekeeper a creature whom I well knew to be silent and unscrupulous. On the other side, I announced to my servants that a Mr. Hyde (whom I described) was to have full liberty and power about my house in the square; and, to parry mishaps, I even called and made myself a familiar object in my second character. I next drew up that will to which you so much objected; so that if anything befell me in the person of Dr. Jekyll, I could enter on that of Edward Hyde without pecuniary loss. And thus fortified, as I supposed, on every side, I began to profit by the strange immunities of my position.

Men have before hired bravos to transact their crimes, while their own person and reputation sat under shelter. I was the first that ever did so for his pleasures. I was the first that could thus plod in the public eye with a load of genial respectability, and in a moment, like a schoolboy, strip off these lendings and spring headlong into the sea of liberty.[2] But for me, in my impenetrable mantle, the safety was complete. Think of it—I did not even exist! Let me but escape into my laboratory door, give me but a second or two to mix and swallow the draught that I had always standing ready; and, whatever he had done, Edward Hyde would pass away like the stain of breath upon a mirror; and there in his stead, quietly at home, trimming the midnight lamp in his study, a man who could afford to laugh at suspicion, would be Henry Jekyll.

The pleasures which I made haste to seek in my disguise were, as I have said, undignified; I would scarce use a harder term. But in the hands of Edward Hyde they soon began to turn towards the monstrous. When I would come back from these excursions, I was often plunged into a kind of wonder at my vicarious depravity. This familiar that I called out of my own soul, and sent forth alone to do his good pleasure, was a being inherently malign and villainous; his every act and thought centred on self; drinking pleasure with bestial avidity from any degree of torture to another; relentless like a man of stone. Henry Jekyll stood at times aghast before the acts of Edward Hyde; but the situation was apart from ordinary laws, and insidiously relaxed the grasp of conscience. It was Hyde, after all, and Hyde alone, that was guilty. Jekyll was no worse; he woke again to his good qualities seemingly unimpaired; he would even make haste, where it was possible, to undo the evil done by Hyde. And thus his conscience slumbered.

Into the details of the infamy at which I thus connived (for even now I can scarce grant that I committed it) I have no design of entering. I mean but to point out the warnings and the successive steps with which my chastisement approached. I met with one accident which, as it brought on no consequence, I shall no more than mention. An act of cruelty to a child aroused against me the anger of a passerby, whom I recognised the other day in the person of your kinsman; the doctor and the child's family joined him; there were moments when I feared for my life; and at last, in order to pacify their too just resentment, Edward Hyde had to bring them to the door, and pay them in a cheque drawn in the name of Henry Jekyll. But this danger was easily eliminated from the future by opening an account at another bank in the name of Edward Hyde himself; and when, by sloping my own hand backwards, I had supplied my double with a signature, I thought I sat beyond the reach of fate.

Some two months before the murder of Sir Danvers, I had been out for one of my adventures, had returned at a late hour, and woke the next day in bed with somewhat odd sensations. It was in vain I looked about me; in vain I saw the decent furniture and tall proportions of my room in the square; in vain that I recognised the pattern of the bed curtains and the design of the mahogany frame; something still kept insisting that I was not where I was, that I had not wakened where I seemed to be, but in the little room in Soho where I was accustomed to sleep in the body of Edward Hyde. I smiled to myself, and, in my psychological way, began lazily to inquire into the elements of this illusion, occasionally, even as I did so, dropping back into a comfortable morning doze. I was still so engaged when, in one of my more wakeful moments, my eye fell upon my hand. Now, the hand of Henry Jekyll (as you have often remarked) was professional in shape and size; it was large, firm, white and comely. But the hand which I now saw, clearly enough in the yellow light of a mid-London morning, lying half shut on the bed-clothes, was lean, corded, knuckly, of a dusky pallor, and thickly shaded with a swart growth of hair. It was the hand of Edward Hyde.

I must have stared upon it for near half a minute, sunk as I was in the mere stupidity of wonder, before terror woke up in my breast as sudden and startling as the crash of cymbals; and bounding from my bed, I rushed to the mirror. At the sight that met my eyes, my blood was changed into something exquisitely thin and icy. Yes, I had gone to bed Henry Jekyll, I had awakened Edward Hyde. How was this to be explained? I asked myself; and then, with another bound of terror—how was it to be remedied? It was well on in the morning; the servants were up; all my drugs were in the cabinet—a long journey, down two pairs of stairs, through the back passage, across the open court and through the anatomical theatre, from where I was then standing horror-struck. It might indeed be possible to cover my face; but of what use was that, when I was unable to conceal the alteration in my stature? And then, with an overpowering sweetness of relief, it came back upon my mind that the servants were already used to the coming and going of my second self. I had soon dressed, as well as I was able, in clothes of my own size; had soon passed through the house, where Bradshaw stared and drew back at seeing Mr. Hyde at such an hour and in such a strange array; and ten minutes later, Dr. Jekyll had returned to his own shape and was sitting down, with a darkened brow, to make a feint of breakfasting.

Small indeed was my appetite. This inexplicable incident, this reversal of my previous experience, seemed, like the Babylonian finger on the wall, to be spelling out the letters of my judgment;[3] and I began to reflect more seriously than ever before on the issues and possibilities of my double existence. That part of me which I had the power of projecting had lately been much exercised and nourished; it had seemed to me of late as though the body of Edward Hyde had grown in stature, as though (when I wore that form) I were conscious of a more generous tide of blood; and I began to spy a danger that, if this were much prolonged, the balance of my nature might be permanently overthrown, the power of voluntary change be forfeited, and the character of Edward Hyde become irrevocably mine. The power of the drug had not been always equally displayed. Once, very early in my career, it had totally failed me; since then I had been obliged on more than one occasion to double, and once, with infinite risk of death, to treble the amount; and these rare uncertainties had cast hitherto the sole shadow on my contentment. Now, however, and in the light of that morning's accident, I was led to remark that whereas, in the beginning, the difficulty had been to throw off the body of Jekyll, it had of late gradually but decidedly transferred itself to the other side. All things therefore seemed to point to this: that I was slowly losing hold of my original and better self, and becoming slowly incorporated with my second and worse.

Between these two I now felt I had to choose. My two natures had memory in common, but all other faculties were most unequally shared between them. Jekyll (who was a composite) now with the most sensitive apprehensions, now with a greedy gusto, projected and shared in the pleasures and adventures of Hyde; but Hyde was indifferent to Jekyll, or but remembered him as the mountain bandit remembers the cavern in which he conceals himself from pursuit. Jekyll had more than a father's interest; Hyde had more than a son's indifference. To cast in my lot with Jekyll was to die to those appetites which I had long secretly indulged and had of late begun to pamper. To cast it in with Hyde was to die to a thousand interests and aspirations, and to become, at a blow and forever, despised and friendless. The bargain might appear unequal; but there was still another consideration in the scales; for while Jekyll would suffer smartingly in the fires of abstinence, Hyde would be not even conscious of all that he had lost. Strange as my circumstances were, the terms of this debate are as old and commonplace as man; much the same inducements and alarms cast the die for any tempted and trembling sinner; and it fell out with me, as it falls with so vast a majority of my fellows, that I chose the better part and was found wanting in the strength to keep to it.

Yes, I preferred the elderly and discontented doctor, surrounded by friends and cherishing honest hopes; and bade a resolute farewell to the liberty, the comparative youth, the light step, leaping pulses and secret pleasures, that I had enjoyed in the disguise of Hyde. I made this choice perhaps with some unconscious reservation, for I neither gave up the house in Soho, nor destroyed the clothes of Edward Hyde, which still lay ready in my cabinet. For two months, however, I was true to my determination; for two months

I led a life of such severity as I had never before attained to, and enjoyed the compensations of an approving conscience. But time began at last to obliterate the freshness of my alarm; the praises of conscience began to grow into a thing of course; I began to be tortured with throes and longings, as of Hyde struggling after freedom; and at last, in an hour of moral weakness, I once again compounded and swallowed the transforming draught.

I do not suppose that when a drunkard reasons with himself upon his vice, he is once out of five hundred times affected by the dangers that he runs through his brutish physical insensibility; neither had I, long as I had considered my position, made enough allowance for the complete moral insensibility and insensate readiness to evil which were the leading characters of Edward Hyde. Yet it was by these that I was punished. My devil had been long caged, he came out roaring. I was conscious, even when I took the draught, of a more unbridled, a more furious propensity to ill. It must have been this, I suppose, that stirred in my soul that tempest of impatience with which I listened to the civilities of my unhappy victim; I declare at least, before God, no man morally sane could have been guilty of that crime upon so pitiful a provocation; and that I struck in no more reasonable spirit than that in which a sick child may break a plaything. But I had voluntarily stripped myself of all those balancing instincts by which even the worst of us continues to walk with some degree of steadiness among temptations; and in my case, to be tempted, however slightly, was to fall.

Instantly the spirit of hell awoke in me and raged. With a transport of glee, I mauled the unresisting body, tasting delight from every blow; and it was not till weariness had begun to succeed that I was suddenly, in the top fit of my delirium, struck through the heart by a cold thrill of terror. A mist dispersed; I saw my life to be forfeit; and fled from the scene of these excesses, at once glorying and trembling, my lust of evil gratified and stimulated, my love of life screwed to the topmost peg. I ran to the house in Soho, and (to make assurance doubly sure) destroyed my papers; thence I set out through the lamplit streets, in the same divided ecstasy of mind, gloating on my crime, light-headedly devising others in the future, and yet still hastening and still harkening in my wake for the steps of the avenger. Hyde had a song upon his lips as he compounded the draught, and as he drank it pledged the dead man. The pangs of transformation had not done tearing him, before Henry Jekyll, with streaming tears of gratitude and remorse, had fallen upon his knees and lifted his clasped hand to God. The veil of self-indulgence was rent from head to foot, I saw my life as a whole: I followed it up from the days of childhood, when I had walked with my father's hand, and through the self-denying toils of my professional life, to arrive again and again, with the same sense of unreality, at the damned horrors of the evening. I could have screamed aloud; I sought with tears and prayers to smother down the crowd of hideous images and sounds with which my memory swarmed against me; and still, between the petitions, the ugly face of my iniquity stared into my soul. As the acuteness of this remorse began to die away, it was succeeded by a sense of joy. The problem of my conduct was solved. Hyde was henceforth impossible; whether I would or not, I was now confined to the better part of my existence; and, oh, how I rejoiced to think it! with what willing humility I embraced anew the restrictions of natural life! with what sincere renunciation I locked the door by which I had so often gone and come, and ground the key under my heel!

The next day came the news that the murder had been overlooked, that the guilt of Hyde was patent to the world, and that the victim was a man high in public estimation. It was not only a crime, it had been a tragic folly. I think I was glad to know it; I think I was glad to have my better impulses thus buttressed and guarded by the terrors of the scaffold. Jekyll was now my city of refuge; let but Hyde peep out an instant, and the hands of all men would be raised to take and slay him.

I resolved in my future conduct to redeem the past; and I can say with honesty that my resolve was fruitful of some good. You know yourself how earnestly in the last months of last year I laboured to relieve suffering; you know that much was done for others, and that the days passed quietly, almost happily for myself. Nor can I truly say that I wearied of this beneficent and innocent life; I think instead that I daily enjoyed it more completely; but I was still cursed with my duality of purpose; and as the first edge of my penitence wore off, the lower side of me, so long indulged, so recently chained down, began to growl for licence. Not that I dreamed of resuscitating Hyde; the bare idea of that would startle me to frenzy: no, it was in my own person that I was once more tempted to trifle with my conscience; and it was as an ordinary secret sinner that I at last fell before the assaults of temptation.

There comes an end to all things; the most capacious measure is filled at last; and this brief condescension to my evil finally destroyed the balance of my soul. And yet I was not alarmed; the fall seemed natural, like a return to the old days before I had made my discovery. It was a fine, clear January day, wet under foot where the frost had melted, but cloudless overhead; and the Regent's Park was full of winter chirrupings and sweet with Spring odours. I sat in the sun on a bench; the animal within me licking the chops of memory; the spiritual side a little drowsed, promising subsequent penitence, but not yet moved to begin. After all, I reflected, I was like my neighbours; and then I smiled, comparing myself with other men, comparing my active good-will with the lazy cruelty of their neglect. And at the very moment of that vainglorious thought, a qualm came over me, a horrid nausea and the most deadly shuddering. These passed away, and left me faint; and then as in its turn the faintness subsided, I began to be aware of a change in the temper of my thoughts, a greater boldness, a contempt of danger, a solution of the bonds of obligation. I looked down; my clothes hung form-lessly on my shrunken limbs; the hand that lay on my knee was corded and hairy. I was once more Edward Hyde. A moment before I had been safe of all men's respect, wealthy, beloved—the cloth laying for me in the dining-room at home; and now I was the common quarry of mankind, hunted, houseless, a known murderer, thrall to the gallows.

My reason wavered, but it did not fail me utterly. I have more than once observed that, in my second character, my faculties seemed sharpened to a point and my spirits more tensely elastic; thus it came about that, where Jekyll perhaps might have suc-cumbed, Hyde rose to the importance of the moment. My drugs were in one of the presses of my cabinet: how was I to reach them? That was the problem that (crushing my temples in my hands) I set myself to solve. The laboratory door I had closed. If I sought to enter by the house, my own servants would consign me to the gallows. I saw I must employ another hand, and thought of Lanyon. How was he to be reached? how persuaded? Supposing that I escaped capture in the streets, how was I to make my way into his presence? and how should I, an unknown and displeasing visitor, prevail on the famous physician to rifle the study of his colleague, Dr. Jekyll? Then I remembered that of my original character, one part remained to me: I could write my own hand; and once I had conceived that kindling spark, the way that I must follow became lighted up from end to end.

Thereupon, I arranged my clothes as best I could, and sum- moning a passing hansom, drove to an hotel in Portland Street, the name of which I chanced to remember. At my appearance (which was indeed comical enough, however tragic a fate these garments covered) the driver could not conceal his mirth. I gnashed my teeth upon him with a gust of devilish fury; and the smile withered from his face—happily for him—yet more happily for myself, for in another instant I had certainly dragged him from his perch. At the inn, as I entered, I looked about me with so black a countenance as made the attendants tremble; not a look did they exchange in my presence; but obsequiously took my orders, led me to a private room, and brought me where- withal to write. Hyde in danger of his life was a creature new to me: shaken with inordinate anger, strung to the pitch of murder, lusting to inflict pain. Yet the creature was astute; mastered his fury with a great effort of the will; composed his two important letters, one to Lanyon and one to Poole, and, that he might receive actual evidence of their being posted, sent them out with directions that they should be registered.

Thenceforward, he sat all day over the fire in the private room, gnawing his nails; there he dined, sitting alone with his fears, the waiter visibly quailing before his eye; and thence, when the night was fully come, he set forth in the corner of a closed cab, and was driven to and fro about the streets of the city. He, I say—I cannot say, I. That child of Hell had nothing human; nothing lived in him but fear and hatred. And when at last, thinking the driver had begun to grow suspicious, he discharged the cab and ventured on foot, attired in his misfitting clothes, an object marked out for observation, into the midst of the nocturnal passengers, these two base passions raged within him like a tempest. He walked fast, hunted by his fears, chattering to himself, skulking through the less frequented thoroughfares, counting the minutes that still divided him from midnight. Once a woman spoke to him, offering, I think, a box of lights. He smote her in the face, and she fled.

When I came to myself at Lanyon's, the horror of my old friend perhaps affected me somewhat: I do not know; it was at least but a drop in the sea to the abhorrence with which I looked back upon these hours. A change had come over me. It was no longer the fear of the gallows, it was the horror of being Hyde that racked me. I received Lanyon's condemnation partly in a dream; it was partly in a dream that I came home to my own house and got into bed. I slept after the prostration of the day, with a stringent and profound slumber which not even the nightmares that wrung me could avail to break. I awoke in the morning shaken, weakened, but refreshed. I still hated and feared the thought of the brute that slept within me, and I had not of course forgotten the appalling dangers of the day before; but I was once more at home, in my own house and close to my drugs; and gratitude for my escape shone so strong in my soul that it almost rivalled the brightness of hope.

I was stepping leisurely across the court after breakfast, drinking the chill of the air with pleasure, when I was seized again with those indescribable sensations that heralded the change; and I had but the time to gain the shelter of my cabinet, before I was once again raging and freezing with the passions of Hyde. It took on this occasion a double dose to recall me to myself; and alas, six hours after, as I sat looking sadly in the fire, the pangs returned, and the drug had to be re-administered. In short, from that day forth it seemed only by a great effort as of gymnastics, and only under the immediate stimulation of the drug, that I was able to wear the countenance of Jekyll. At all hours of the day and night I would be taken with the premonitory shudder; above all, if I slept, or even dozed for a moment in my chair, it was always as Hyde that I awakened. Under the strain of this continually impending doom and by the sleeplessness to which I now condemned myself, ay, even beyond what I had thought possible to man, I became, in my own person, a creature eaten up and emptied by fever, languidly weak both in body and mind, and solely occupied by one thought: the horror of my other self. But when I slept, or when the virtue of the medicine wore off, I would leap almost without transition (for the pangs of transformation grew daily less marked) into the possession of a fancy brimming with images of terror, a soul boiling with causeless hatreds, and a body that seemed not strong enough to contain the raging energies of life. The powers of Hyde seemed to have grown with the sickliness of Jekyll. And certainly the hate that now divided them was equal on each side. With Jekyll, it was a thing of vital instinct. He had now seen the full deformity of that creature that shared with him some of the phenomena of consciousness, and was co-heir with him to death: and beyond these links of community, which in themselves made the most poignant part of his distress, he thought of Hyde, for all his energy of life, as of something not only hellish but inorganic. This was the shocking thing; that the slime of the pit seemed to utter cries and voices; that the amorphous dust gesticulated and sinned; that what was dead, and had no shape, should usurp the offices of life. And this again, that that insurgent horror was knit to him closer than a wife, closer than an eye; lay caged in his flesh, where he heard it mutter and felt it struggle to be born; and at every hour of weakness, and in the confidences of slumber, prevailed against him, and deposed him out of life. The hatred of Hyde for Jekyll was of a different order. His terror of the gallows drove him continually to commit temporary suicide, and return to his subordinate station of a part instead of a person; but he loathed the necessity, he loathed the despondency into which Jekyll was now fallen, and he resented the dislike with which he was himself regarded. Hence the ape-like tricks that he would play me, scrawling in my own hand blasphemies on the pages of my books, burning the letters and destroying the portrait of my father; and indeed, had it not been for his fear of death, he would long ago have ruined himself in order to involve me in the ruin.

But his love of life is wonderful; I go further: I, who sicken and freeze at the mere thought of him, when I recall the abjection and passion of this attachment, and when I know how he fears my power to cut him off by suicide, I find it in my heart to pity him.

It is useless, and the time awfully fails me, to prolong this description; no one has ever suffered such torments, let that suffice; and yet even to these, habit brought—no, not alleviation—but a certain callousness of soul, a certain acquiescence of despair, and my punishment might have gone on for years, but for the last calamity which has now fallen, and which has finally severed me from my own face and nature. My provision of the salt, which had never been renewed since the date of the first experiment, began to run low. I sent out for a fresh supply, and mixed the draught; the ebullition followed, and the first change of colour, not the second; I drank it, and it was without efficiency. You will learn from Poole how I have had London ransacked; it was in vain; and I am now persuaded that my first supply was impure, and that it was that unknown impurity which lent efficacy to the draught.

About a week has passed, and I am now finishing this statement under the influence of the last of the old powders. This, then, is the last time, short of a miracle, that Henry Jekyll can think his own thoughts or see his own face (now how sadly altered!) in the glass. Nor must I delay too long to bring my writing to an end; for if my narrative has hitherto escaped destruction, it has been by a combination of great prudence and great good luck. Should the throes of change take me in the act of writing it, Hyde will tear it in pieces; but if some time shall have elapsed after I have laid it by, his wonderful selfishness and circumscription to the moment will probably save it once again from the action of his ape-like spite. And indeed the doom that is closing on us both has already changed and crushed him. Half an hour from now, when I shall again and for ever reindue that hated personality, I know how I shall sit shuddering and weeping in my chair, or continue, with the most strained and fearstruck ecstasy of listening, to pace up and down this room (my last earthly refuge) and give ear to every sound of menace. Will Hyde die upon the scaffold? or will he find the courage to release himself at the last moment? God knows; I am careless; this is my true hour of death, and what

is to follow concerns another than myself. Here, then, as I lay
down the pen, and proceed to seal up my confession, I bring the
life of that unhappy Henry Jekyll to an end.

Notes

1 Jekyll's ironic memory of a salvation recounted in *Acts* 16. Evangeliz-
ing in Philippi, Paul and his followers are beaten, cast into prison, and
bound in stocks. At midnight an earthquake shakes the prison doors
open and loosens the prisoner's bands. The prison-keeper is about to
commit suicide on supposing the prisoners have all escaped, but he is
converted by Paul; the next day all are released.

2 Shocked at the sight of ragged beggar "poor Tom," and startled into the
recognition that man is basically "no more but such a poor, bare, forked
animal," King Lear tears off his clothes, crying out "Off, off you lendings!"
(Shakespeare, *King Lear* III.iv). Stevenson also echoes a comment in a letter
by the poet John Keats, on whose biography Stevenson's friend, Sidney
Colvin, was working (it would be published the year after *Jekyll and
Hyde*, in 1887). Keats had devoted himself to a long poem, *Endymion*,
with great hopes of success, but by the time it was published he
regarded it as "slip-shod" and was more than confirmed by mean-spir-
ited, ridiculing reviews. "Had I been nervous about it being a perfect
piece, and with that view asked advice, and trembled over every page, it
would not have been written," he wrote to his publisher, adding, "In
Endymion, I leaped headlong into the sea, and thereby have become better
acquainted with the soundings, the quicksands, and the rocks, than if I
had stayed upon the green shore, and piped a silly pipe, and took tea
and comfortable advice" (8 October 1818, from *Life, Letters, and Literary
Remains of John Keats*, 1848). For Keats, the headlong leap is not a bursting
out of prison but a venture into perilous liberty. Jekyll echoes both
Keats's contempt for a safe, timid life and Lear's recognition of humanity's
elemental character as creatures vulnerable to nature.

3 The feast of Belshazzar, king of Babylonia (the book of *Daniel*), is thrown
into disruption when there "came forth fingers of a man's hand, and wrote
. . . upon the plaister of the wall." Daniel, famed for his powers of "inter-
pretation," reads the mysterious words as meaning "God hath numbered
thy kingdom, and finished it. . . . Thou art weighed in the balances, and art
found wanting. . . . Thy kingdom is divided and given to the Medes and
Persians" (*Daniel* 5.5, 18–28).

Robert Louis Stevenson
on
The Strange Case of Dr. Jekyll and Mr. Hyde

LETTER TO W. H. LOW, 2 JANUARY 1886

I send you herewith a Gothic gnome for your Greek nymph; but the gnome is interesting, I think, and he came out of a deep mine, where he guards the fountain of tears. It is not always the time to rejoice.—
Yours ever,

R. L. S.

The gnome's name is *Jekyll & Hyde*; I believe you will find he is likewise quite willing to answer to the name of Low or Stevenson.

LETTER TO J. A. SYMONDS, SPRING 1886

Jekyll is a dreadful thing, I own; but the only thing I feel dreadful about is that damned old business of the war in the members. This time it came out; I hope it will stay in, in future.

LETTER TO JOHN PAUL BOCOCK, NOVEMBER 1887

Your prominent dramatic critic, writing like a journalist, has written like a braying ass: what he meant is probably quite different and true enough—that the work is ugly and the allegory too like the usual pulpit judge and not just enough to the modesty of facts. You are right as to Mansfield: Hyde was the younger of the two. He was not good looking however; and not, great gods! a mere voluptuary. There is no harm in a voluptuary; and none, with my hand on my heart and in the sight of God, none—no harm whatever—in what prurient fools call 'immorality.' The harm was in Jekyll, because he was a hypocrite—not because he was fond of women; he says so himself; but people are so filled full of folly and inverted lust, that they can think of nothing but sexuality. The hypocrite let out the beast Hyde—who is no more sensual than another, but who is the essence of cruelty and malice, and selfishness and cowardice: and these are the diabolic in man—not this poor wish to have a woman, that they make such a cry about. I know, and I dare to say, you know as well as I, that bad and good, even to our human eyes, has no more connection with what is called dissipation than it has with flying kites. But the sexual field and the business field are perhaps the two best fitted for the display of cruelty and cowardice and selfishness. That is what people see; and then they confound.

from "A CHAPTER ON DREAMS" (1892)

I can but give an instance or so of what part is done sleeping and what part awake, and leave the reader to share what laurels there are, at his own nod, between myself and my collaborators; and to do this I will first take a book that a number of persons have been polite enough to read, *The Strange Case of Dr. Jekyll and Mr. Hyde*. I had long been trying to write a story on this subject, to find a body, a vehicle, for that strong sense of man's double being which must at times come in upon and overwhelm the mind of every thinking creature. I had even written one, *The Travelling Companion*, which was returned by an editor on the plea that it was a work of genius and indecent, and which I burned the other day on the ground that it was not a work of genius, and that *Jekyll* had supplanted it. Then came one of those financial fluctuations to which (with an elegant modesty) I have hitherto referred in the third person. For two days I went about racking my brains for a plot of any sort; and on the second night I dreamed the scene at the window, and a scene afterward split in two, in which Hyde, pursued for some crime, took the powder and underwent the change in the presence of his pursuers. All the rest was made awake, and consciously, although I think I can trace in much of it the manner of my Brownies. The meaning of the tale is therefore mine, and had long pre-existed in my garden of Adonis, and tried one body after another in vain; indeed, I do most of the morality, worse luck! and my Brownies have not a rudiment of what we call a conscience. Mine, too, is the setting, mine the characters. All that was given me was the matter of three scenes, and the central idea of a voluntary change becoming involuntary. Will it be thought ungenerous, after I have been so liberally ladling out praise to my unseen collaborators, if I here toss them over, bound hand and foot, into the arena of the critics? For the business of the powders, which so many have censured, is, I am relieved to say, not mine at all but the Brownies'. Of another tale, in case the reader should have glanced at it, I may say a word: the not very defensible story of *Olalla*. Here the court, the mother, the mother's niche, Olalla, Olalla's chamber, the meetings on the stair, the broken window, the ugly scene of the bite, were all given me in bulk and detail as I have tried to write them; to this I added only the external scenery (for in my dream I never was beyond the court), the portrait, the characters of Felipe and the priest, the moral, such as it is, and the last pages, such as, alas! they are. And I may even say that in this case the moral itself was given me; for it arose immediately on a comparison of the mother and the daughter, and from the hideous trick of atavism in the first. Sometimes a parabolic sense is still more undeniably present in a dream; sometimes I cannot but suppose my Brownies have been aping Bunyan, and yet in no case with what would possibly be called a moral in a tract; never with the ethical narrowness; conveying hints instead of life's larger limitations and that sort of sense which we seem to perceive in the arabesque of time and space.

For the most part, it will be seen, my Brownies[1] are somewhat fantastic, like their stories hot and hot, full of passion and the picturesque, alive with animating incident; and they have no prejudice against the supernatural. But the other day they gave me a surprise, entertaining me with a love story, a little April comedy, which I ought certainly to hand over to the author of *A Chance Acquaintance*, for he could write it as it should be written, and I am sure (although I mean to try) that I cannot.—But who would have supposed that a Brownie of mine should invent a tale for Mr. Howells?

Note

[1] A "wee brown man" often appears in Scottish ballads and fairy tales. In folk tradition, a Brownie is a benevolent spirit or goblin, of shaggy appearance, supposed to haunt old houses, especially farmhouses, in Scotland, and sometimes to perform useful household work while the family is asleep. (Oxford English Dictionary)

The Critics Speak
1886–1990

- Andrew Lang, *Saturday Review*, 9 January 1886
- James Ashcroft Noble, *Academy*, 23 January 1886
- *The Times*, 25 January 1886
- J. A. Symonds: Letter to Stevenson, 3 March 1886
- Julia Wedgwood, *Contemporary Review*, April 1886
- Gerard Manley Hopkins: Letter to Robert Bridges, 28 October 1886
- Henry James, *Partial Portraits*, 1888
- Oscar Wilde, *The Decay of Lying*, 1889
- G. K. Chesterton, *Robert Louis Stevenson*, 1928
- Vladimir Nabokov, 1950s
- Leslie Fiedler, 1963
- Edwin Eigner, 1966
- Masao Miyoshi, 1969
- Jorge Luis Borges, 1973
- Irving Sposnik, 1974
- Stephen Heath, 1986
- Patrick Brantlinger and Richard Boyle, 1988
- Peter K. Garrett, 1988
- Ronald R. Thomas, 1988
- William Veeder, 1988
- Elaine Showalter, 1990
- Joyce Carol Oates, 1990

The Critics Speak
1886–1990

ANDREW LANG

(*SATURDAY REVIEW*, 9 JANUARY 1886)

Mr. Stevenson's *Prince Otto* was, no doubt, somewhat disappointing to many of his readers. They will be hard to please if they are disappointed in his *Strange Case of Dr. Jekyll and Mr. Hyde*. To adopt a recent definition of some of Mr. Stevenson's tales, this little shilling work is like "Poe with the addition of a moral sense." Or perhaps to say that would be to ignore the fact that Poe was extremely fond of one kind of moral, of allegories in which embodied Conscience plays its part with terrible efficacy. The tale of *William Wilson*, and perhaps that of the *Tell-Tale Heart*, are examples of Poe in this humour. Now Mr. Stevenson's narrative is not, of course, absolutely original in idea. Probably we shall never see a story that in germ is absolutely original. The very rare possible germinal conceptions of romance appear to have been picked up and appropriated by the very earliest masters of fiction. But the possible combinations and possible methods of treatment are infinite, and all depends on how the ideas are treated and combined.

Mr. Stevenson's idea, his secret (but a very open secret) is that of the double personality in every man. The mere conception is familiar enough. Poe used it in *William Wilson* and Gautier in *Le Chevalier Double*. Yet Mr. Stevenson's originality of treatment remains none the less striking and astonishing. The double personality does not in his romance take the form of a personified conscience, the *doppel ganger* of the sinner, a "double" like his own double which Goethe is fabled to have seen. No; the "separable self" in this "strange case" is all unlike that in *William Wilson*, and, with its unlikeness to its master, with its hideous caprices, and appalling vitality, and terrible power of growth and increase, is, to our thinking, a notion as novel as it is terrific. We would welcome a spectre, a ghoul, or even a vampire gladly, rather than meet Mr. Edward Hyde. Without telling the whole story, and to some extent spoiling the effect, we cannot explain the exact nature of the relations between Jekyll and Hyde, nor reveal the mode (itself, we think, original, though it depends on resources of pseudoscience) in which they were developed. Let it suffice to say that Jekyll's emotions when, as he sits wearily in the park, he finds that his hand is not his own hand, but another's; and that other moment when Utterson, the lawyer, is brought to Jekyll's door, and learns that his locked room is haunted by something which moans and weeps; and, again, the process beheld by Dr. Lanyon, are all of them as terrible as anything ever dreamed of by Poe. They lack, too, that quality of merely earthly horror or of physical corruption and decay which Poe was apt to introduce so frequently and with such unpleasant and unholy enjoyment.

It is a proof of Mr. Stevenson's skill that he has chosen the scene for his wild "Tragedy of a Body and a Soul," as it might have been called, in the most ordinary and respectable quarters of London. His heroes (surely *this* is original) are all successful middle-aged professional men. No woman appears in the tale (as in *Treasure Island*, and we incline to think that Mr. Stevenson always does himself most justice in novels without a heroine. It may be regarded by some critics as a drawback to the tale that it inevitably disengages a powerful lesson in conduct. It is not a moral allegory, of course; but you cannot help reading the moral into it, and recognizing that, just as every one of us, according to Mr. Stevenson, travels through life with a donkey (as he himself did in the Cévennes), so every Jekyll among us is haunted by his own Hyde. But it would be most unfair to insist on this, as there is nothing a novel-reader hates more than to be done good to unawares. Nor has Mr. Stevenson, obviously, any didactic purpose. The moral of the tale is its natural soul, and no more separable from it than, in ordinary life, Hyde is separable from Jekyll.

While one is thrilled and possessed by the horror of the central fancy, one may fail, at first reading, to recognize the delicate and restrained skill of the treatment of accessories, details, and character. Mr. Utterson, for example, Jekyll's friend, is an admirable portrait, and might occupy a place unchallenged among pictures by the best masters of sober fiction.

> At friendly meetings, and when the wine was to his taste, something eminently human beaconed from his eye; something indeed which never found its way into his talk; but which spoke not only in these silent symbols of the after-dinner face, but more often and loudly in the acts of his life. He was austere with himself, but tolerant to others, sometimes wondering, almost with envy, at the high pressure of spirits involved in their misdeeds.

It is fair to add that, while the style of the new romance is usually as plain as any style so full of compressed thought and incident can be, there is at least one passage in the threshold of the book where Mr. Stevenson yields to his old Tempter, "preciousness." Nay, we cannot restrain the fancy that, if the good and less good of Mr. Stevenson's literary personality could be divided like Dr. Jekyll's moral and physical personality, his literary Mr. Hyde would greatly resemble—the reader may fill in the blank at his own will. The idea is capable of development. Perhaps Canon McColl is Mr. Gladstone's Edward Hyde, a solution of historical problems which may be applauded by future generations. This is wandering from the topic in hand. It is pleasant to acknowledge that the half-page of "preciousness" stands almost alone in this excellent and horrific and captivating romance, where Mr. Stevenson gives us of his very best and increases that debt of gratitude which we all owe him for so many and such rare pleasures.

There should be a limited edition of the *Strange Case* on Large Paper. It looks lost in a shilling edition—the only "bob'svorth," as the cabman said when he took up Mr. Pickwick, which has real permanent literary merit.

JAMES ASHCROFT NOBLE
(*ACADEMY*, 23 JANUARY 1886)

The Strange Case of Dr. Jekyll and Mr. Hyde is not an orthodox three-volume novel; it is not even a one-volume novel of the ordinary type; it is simply a paper-covered shilling story, belonging, so far as external appearance goes, to a class of literature familiarity with which has bred in the minds of most readers a certain measure of contempt. Appearances, it has been once or twice remarked, are deceitful; and in this case they are very deceitful indeed, for, in spite of the paper cover and the popular price, Mr. Stevenson's story distances so unmistakably its three-volume and one-volume competitors, that its only fitting place is the place of honour. It is, indeed, many years since English fiction has been enriched by any work at once so weirdly imaginative in conception and so faultlessly ingenious in construction as this little tale, which can be read with ease in a couple of hours. Dr. Henry Jekyll is a medical man of high reputation, not only as regards his professional skill, but his general moral and social character; and this reputation is, in the main, well-deserved, for he has honourable instincts and high aspirations with which the greater part of his life of conduct is in harmony. He has also, however, "a certain impatient gaiety of disposition," which at times impels him to indulge in pleasures of a kind which, while they would bring to many men no sense of shame, and therefore no prompting to concealment, do bring to him such sense and such prompting, in virtue of their felt inconsistency with the visible tenor of his existence. The divorce between the two lives becomes so complete that he is haunted and tortured by the consciousness of a double identity which deprives each separate life of its full measure of satisfaction. It is at this point that he makes a wonderful discovery, which seems to cut triumphantly the knot of his perplexity. The discovery is of certain chemical agents, the application of which can give the needed wholeness and homogeneity of individuality by destroying for a time all consciousness of one set of conflicting impulses, so that when the experimenter pleases his lower instincts can absorb his whole being, and, knowing nothing of restraint from anything above them, manifest themselves in new and quite diabolical activities. But this is not all. The fateful drug acts with its strange transforming power upon the body as well as the mind; for when the first dose has been taken the unhappy victim finds that "soul is form and doth the body make," and that his new nature, of evil all compact, has found for itself a corresponding environment, the shrunken shape and loathsome expression of which bear no resemblance to the shape and expression of Dr. Jekyll. It is this monster who appears in the world as Mr. Hyde, a monster whose play is outrage and murder; but who, though known, can never be captured, because when he is apparently traced to the doctor's house, no one is found there but the benevolent and highly honoured doctor himself. The re-transformation has, of course, been affected by another dose of the drug; but as time goes by Dr. Jekyll notices a curious and fateful change in its operation. At first the dethronement of the higher nature has been difficult; sometimes a double portion of the chemical agent has been found necessary to bring about the result; but the lower nature gains a vitality of its own, and at times the transformation from Jekyll to Hyde takes place without any preceding act of volition. How the story ends I must not say. Too much of it has already been told; but without something of such telling it would have been impossible to write an intelligible review. And, indeed, the story has a much larger and deeper interest than that belonging to a mere skilful narrative. It is a marvellous exploration into the recesses of human nature; and though it is more than possible that Mr. Stevenson wrote with no ethical intent, its impressiveness as a parable is equal to its fascination as a work of art. I do not ignore the many differences between the genius of the author of *The Scarlet Letter* and that of the author of *Dr. Jekyll and Mr. Hyde* when I say that the latter story is worthy of Hawthorne.

THE TIMES
(25 JANUARY 1886)

Nothing Mr. Stevenson has written as yet has so strongly impressed us with the versatility of his very original genius as this sparsely-printed little shilling volume. From the business point of view we can only marvel in these practical days at the lavish waste of admirable material, and what strikes us as a disproportionate expenditure on brain-power, in relation to the tangible results. Of two things, one. Either the story was a flash of intuitive psychological research, dashed off in a burst of inspiration; or else it is the product of the most elaborate forethought, fitting together all the parts of an intricate and inscrutable puzzle. The proof is, that every connoisseur who reads the story once, must certainly read it twice. He will read it the first time, passing from surprise to surprise, in a curiosity that keeps growing, because it is never satisfied. For the life of us, we cannot make out how such and such an incident can possibly be explained on grounds that are intelligible or in any way plausible. Yet all the time the seriousness of the tone assures us that explanations are forthcoming. In our impatience we are hurried towards the denouement, which accounts for everything upon strictly scientific grounds, though the science be the science of problematical futurity. Then, having drawn a sigh of relief at having found even a fantastically speculative issue from our embarrassments, we begin reflectively to call to mind how systematically the writer has been working towards it. Never for a moment, in the most startling situations, has he lost his grasp of the grand ground-facts of a wonderful and supernatural problem. Each apparently incredible or insignificant detail has been thoughtfully subordinated to his purpose. And if we say, after all, on a calm retrospect, that the strange case is absurdly and insanely improbable, Mr. Stevenson might answer in the words of Hamlet, that there are more things in heaven and in earth than are dreamed of in our philosophy. For we are still groping by doubtful lights on the dim limits of boundless investigation; and it is always possible that we may be on the brink of a new revelation as to the unforeseen resources of the medical art. And, at all events, the answer should suffice for the purposes of Mr. Stevenson's sensational *tour d'esprit*.

The Strange Case of Dr. Jekyll is sensational enough in all conscience, and yet we do not promise it the wide popularity of *Called Back*. The *brochure* that brought fame and profit to the late Mr. Fargus was pitched in a more commonplace key, and consequently appealed to more vulgar circles. But, for ourselves, we should many times sooner have the credit of *Dr. Jekyll*, which appeals irresistibly to the most cultivated minds, and must be appreciated by the most competent critics. Naturally, we compare it with the sombre masterpieces of Poe, and we may say at once that Mr. Stevenson has gone far deeper. Poe embroidered richly in the gloomy grandeur of his imagination upon themes that were but too material, and not very novel—on the sinister destiny overshadowing a doomed family, on a living and breathing man kept prisoner in a coffin or vault, on the wild whirling of a human waif in the boiling eddies of the Maelstrom—while Mr. Stevenson evolves the ideas of his story from the world that is unseen, enveloping everything in weird mystery, till at last it pleases him to give us the password. We are not going to tell his strange story, though we might well do so, and only excite the curiosity of our readers. We shall only say that we are shown the shrewdest of lawyers hopelessly puzzled by the inexplicable conduct of a familiar friend. All the antecedents of a life of virtue and honour seem to be belied by the discreditable intimacy that has been formed with one of the most callous and atrocious of criminals. A crime committed under the eyes of a witness goes unavenged, though the notorious criminal has been identified, for he disappears as absolutely as if the earth had swallowed him. He reappears in due time where we should least expect to see him, and for some miserable days he leads a charmed life, while he excites the superstitious terrors of all about him. Indeed, the strongest nerves are shaken by stress of sinister circumstances, as well they may be, for the worthy Dr. Jekyll—the benevolent physician—has likewise vanished amid events that are enveloped in impalpable mysteries; nor can any one surmise what has become of him. So with overwrought feelings and conflicting anticipations we are brought to the end, where all is accounted for, more or less credibly.

Nor is it the mere charm of the story, strange as it is, which fascinates and thrills us. Mr. Stevenson is known for a master of style, and never has he shown his resources more remarkably than on this occasion. We do not mean that the book is written in excellent English—that must be a matter of course; but he has weighed his words and turned his sentences so as to sustain and excite throughout the sense of mystery and of horror. The mere artful use of an "it" for a "he" may go far in that respect, and Mr. Stevenson has carefully chosen his language and missed no opportunity. And if his style is good, his motive is better, and shows a higher order of genius. Slight as is the story, and supremely sensational, we remember nothing better since George Eliot's *Romola* than this delineation of a feeble but kindly nature steadily and inevitably succumbing to the sinister influences of besetting weaknesses. With no formal preaching and without a touch of Pharisaism, he works out the essential power of Evil, which, with its malignant patience and unwearying perseverance, gains ground with each casual yielding to temptation, till the once well-meaning man may actually become a fiend, or at least wear the reflection of the fiend's image. But we have said enough to show our opinion of the book, which should be read as a finished study in the art of fantastic literature.

J. A. SYMONDS
(LETTER TO STEVENSON,
3 MARCH 1886)

My dear Louis

At last I have read *Dr. Jekyll*. It makes me wonder whether a man has the right so to scrutinize "the abysmal deeps of personality." It is indeed a dreadful book, most dreadful because of a certain moral callousness, a want of sympathy, a shutting out of hope. The art is burning and intense. The "Peau de Chagrin" disappears; Poe is as water. As a piece of literary work, this seems to me the finest you have done—in all that regards style, invention, psychological analysis, exquisite fitting of parts, and admirable employment of motives to realize the abnormal. But it has left such a deeply painful impression on my heart that I do not know how I am ever to turn to it again.

The fact is that, viewed as an allegory, it touches one too closely. Most of us at some epoch of our lives have been upon the verge of developing a Mr. Hyde.

Physical and biological Science on a hundred lines is reducing individual freedom to zero, and weakening the sense of responsibility. I doubt whether the artist should lend his genius to this grim argument. Your Dr. Jekyll seems to me capable of loosening the last threads of self-control in one who should read it while wavering between his better and worse self. It is like the Cave of Despair in the *Faery Queen*.

I had the great biologist Lauder Brunton with me a fortnight back. He was talking about Dr. Jekyll and a book by W. O. Holmes, in which atavism is played with. I could see that, though a Christian, he held very feebly to the theory of human liberty; and these two works of fiction interested him, as Dr. Jekyll does me, upon that point at issue.

I understand now thoroughly how much a sprite you are. Really there is something not quite human in your genius!

The denouement would have been finer, I think, if Dr. Jekyll by a last supreme effort of his lucid self had given Mr. Hyde up to justice—which might have been arranged after the scene in Lanyon's study. Did you ever read Raskolnikow [*Crime and Punishment*]? How fine is that ending! Had you made your hero act thus, you would at least have saved the sense of human dignity. The doors of Broadmoor would have closed on Mr. Hyde.

Goodbye. I seem quite to have lost you. But if I come to England I shall try to see you.

Love to your wife.

Everyrs
J. A. Symonds

JULIA WEDGWOOD
(*CONTEMPORARY REVIEW*, APRIL 1886)

By far the most remarkable work we have to notice this time is *The Strange Case of Dr. Jekyll and Mr. Hyde*, a shilling story, which the reader devours in an hour, but to which he may return again and again, to study a profound allegory and admire a model of style. It is a perfectly original production; it recalls, indeed, the work of Hawthorne, but this is by kindred power, not by imitative workmanship. We will not do so much injustice to any possible reader of this weird tale as to describe its motif, but we blunt no curiosity in saying that its motto might have been the sentence of a Latin father—"Omnis anima et rea et testis est." Mr. Stevenson has set before himself the psychical problem of Hawthorne's *Transformation*, viewed from a different and perhaps an opposite point of view, and has dealt with it with more vigour if with less grace. Here it is not the child of Nature who becomes manly by experience of sin, but a fully-developed man who goes through a different form of the process, and if the delineation is less associated with beautiful imagery, the parable is deeper, and, we would venture to add, truer. Mr. Stevenson represents the individualizing influence of modern democracy in its more concentrated form. Whereas most fiction deals with the relation between man and woman (and the very fact that its scope is so much narrowed is a sign of the atomic character of our modern thought), the author of this strange tale takes an even narrower range, and sets himself to investigate the meaning of the word *self*. No woman's name occurs in the book, no romance is even suggested in it; it depends on the interest of an idea; but so powerfully is this interest worked out that the reader feels that the same material might have been spun out to cover double the space, and still have struck him as condensed and close-knit workmanship. It is one of those rare fictions which make one understand the value of temperance in art. If this tribute appears exaggerated, it is at least the estimate of one who began Mr. Stevenson's story with a prejudice against it, arising from a recent perusal of its predecessor, his strangely dull and tasteless

"Prince Otto." It is a psychological curiosity that the same man should have written both, and if they were bound up together, the volume would form the most striking illustration of a warning necessary for others besides the critic—the warning to judge no man by any single utterance, how complete soever.

GERARD MANLEY HOPKINS
(LETTER TO ROBERT BRIDGES,
28 OCTOBER 1886)

Jekyll and Hyde I have read. You speak of the "gross absurdity" of the interchange. Enough that it is impossible and might perhaps have been a little better masked: it must be connived at, and it gives rise to a fine situation. It is not more impossible than fairies, giants, heathen gods, and lots of things that literature teems with—and none more than yours. You are certainly wrong about Hyde being overdrawn: my Hyde is worse. The trampling scene is perhaps a convention: he was thinking of something unsuitable for fiction.

I can by no means grant that the characters are not characterised, though how deep the springs of their surface action are I am not yet clear. But the superficial touches of character are admirable: how can you be so blind as not to see them? e.g. Utterson frowning, biting the end of his finger, and saying to the butler "This is a strange tale you tell me, my man, a very strange tale." And Dr. Lanyon: "I used to like it [life], sir; yes, sir, I liked it. Sometimes I think if we knew all" etc. These are worthy of Shakespeare. Have you read the "Pavilion on the Links" in the volume of *Arabian Nights* (not one of them)? The absconding banker is admirably characterised, the horror is nature itself, and the whole piece is genius from beginning to end.

In my judgment the amount of gift and genius which goes into novels in the English literature of this generation is perhaps not much inferior to what made the Elizabethan drama, and unhappily it is in great part wasted. How admirable are Blackmore and Hardy! Their merits are much eclipsed by the overdone reputations of the Evans—Eliot—Lewes—Cross woman [George Elliot] (poor creature! one ought not to speak slightingly, I know), half real power, half imposition. Do you know the bonfire scenes in the *Return of the Native* and still better the sword-exercise scene in the *Madding Crowd*, breathing of epic? or the wife-sale in the *Mayor of Casterbridge* (read by chance)? But these writers only rise to their great strokes; they do not write continuously well: now Stevenson is master of a consummate style, and each phrase is finished as in poetry. It will not do at all, your treatment of him.

HENRY JAMES
(*PARTIAL PORTRAITS*, 1888)

Is *Doctor Jekyll and Mr. Hyde* a work of high philosophic intention, or simply the most ingenious and irresponsible of fictions? It has the stamp of a really imaginative production, that we may take it in different ways; but I suppose it would generally be called the most serious of the author's tales. It deals with the relation of the baser parts of man to his nobler, of the capacity for evil that exists in the most generous natures; and it expresses these things in a fable which is a wonderfully happy invention. The subject is endlessly interesting, and rich in all sorts of provocation, and Mr. Stevenson is to be congratulated on having touched the core of it. I may do him injustice, but it is, however, here, not the profundity of the idea which strikes me so much as the art of the presentation—the extremely successful form. There is a genuine feeling for the perpetual moral question, a fresh sense of the difficulty of being good and the brutishness of being bad; but what there is above all is a singular ability in holding the interest. I confess that that, to my sense, is the most edifying thing in the short, rapid, concentrated story, which is really a masterpiece of concision. There is something almost impertinent in the way, as I have noticed, in which Mr. Stevenson achieves his best effects without the aid of the ladies, and *Doctor Jekyll* is a capital example of his heartless independence. It is usually supposed that a truly poignant impression cannot be made without them, but in the drama of

Mr. Hyde's fatal ascendency, they remain altogether in the wing. It is very obvious—I do not say it cynically—that they must have played an important part in his development. The gruesome tone of the tale is, no doubt, deepened by their absence: it is like the late afternoon light of a foggy winter Sunday, when even inanimate objects have a kind of wicked look. I remember few situations in the pages of mystifying fiction more to the purpose than the episode of Mr. Utterson's going to Doctor Jekyll's to confer with the butler when the Doctor is locked up in his laboratory, and the old servant, whose sagacity has hitherto encountered success-fully the problems of the sideboard and the pantry, confesses that this time he is utterly baffled. The way the two men, at the door of the laboratory, discuss the identity of the mysterious personage inside, who has revealed himself in two or three inhuman glimpses to Poole, has those touches of which irresistible shudders are made. The butler's theory is that his master has been murdered, and that the murderer is in the room, personating him with a sort of clumsy diabolism. "Well, when that masked thing like a monkey jumped from among the chemicals and whipped into the cabinet, it went down my spine like ice." That is the effect upon the reader of most of the story. I say of most rather than of all, because the ice rather melts in the sequel, and I have some diffi-culty in accepting the business of the powders, which seems to me too explicit and explanatory. The powders constitute the machinery of the transformation, and it will probably have struck many readers that this uncanny process would be more conceivable (so far as one may speak of the conceivable in such a case), if the author had not made it so definite.

OSCAR WILDE, *THE DECAY OF LYING*
(*THE NINETEENTH CENTURY*, JANUARY 1889)

VIVIAN: . . . Life imitates art far more than Art imitates life. . . . Literature always anticipates life. . . . Shortly after Mr. Stevenson published his curious psychological story of transformation, a friend of mine, called Mr. Hyde, was in the north of London, and

being anxious to get to a railway station, took what he thought
would be a short cut, lost his way, and found himself in a net-
work of mean, evil-looking streets. Feeling rather nervous he
began to walk extremely fast, when suddenly out of an archway
ran a child right between his legs. It fell on the pavement, he
tripped over it, and trampled upon it. Being, of course, very much
frightened and a little hurt, it began to scream, and in a few seconds
the whole street was full of rough people who came pouring out of
the houses like ants. They surrounded him, and asked him his
name. He was just about to give it when he suddenly remembered
the opening incident in Mr. Stevenson's story. He was so filled with
horror at having realized in his own person that terrible and well-
written scene, and at having done accidentally, though in fact, what
the Mr. Hyde of fiction had done with deliberate intent, that he
ran away as hard as he could go. He was, however, very closely
followed, and finally he took refuge in a surgery, the door of
which happened to be open, where he explained to a young
assistant, who happened to be there, exactly what had occurred.
The humanitarian crowd were induced to go away on his giving
them a small sum of money, and as soon as the coast was clear he
left. As he passed out, the name on the brass door-plate of the
surgery caught his eye. It was "Jekyll." At least it should have been.

G. K. CHESTERTON
(*ROBERT LOUIS STEVENSON*, 1928)

. . . [W]hat is especially to the point of the present argument,
there is a sense in which that Puritanism is expressed even more
in Mr. Hyde than in Dr. Jekyll. The sense of the sudden stink of
evil, the immediate invitation to step into stark filth, the abruptness
of the alternative between that prim and proper pavement and
that black and reeking gutter—all this, though doubtless
involved in the logic of the tale, is far too frankly and familiarly
offered not to have had some basis in observation and reality. . . .
The real stab of the story is not in the discovery that the one man
is two men; but in the discovery that the two men are one man.

After all the diverse wandering and warring of those two incompatible beings, there was still only one man born and only one man buried. . . . The point of the story is not that a man *can* cut himself off from his conscience, but that he cannot. The surgical operation is fatal in the story. It is an amputation of which both the parts die. Jekyll, even in dying, declares the conclusion of the matter; that the load of man's moral struggle cannot be thus escaped. The reason is that there can never be equality between the evil and the good. Jekyll and Hyde are not twin brothers. They are rather, as one of them truly remarks, like father and son. After all, Jekyll created Hyde; Hyde would never have created Jekyll; he only destroyed Jekyll.

VLADIMIR NABOKOV
("THE STRANGE CASE OF
DR. JEKYLL AND MR. HYDE," 1950S)

Stevenson has set himself a difficult artistic problem, and we wonder very much if he is strong enough to solve it. Let us break it up into the following points:

1. In order to make the fantasy plausible he wishes to have it pass through the minds of matter-of-fact persons, Utterson and Enfield, who even for all their commonplace logic must be affected by something bizarre and nightmarish in Hyde.

2. These two stolid souls must convey to the reader something of the horror of Hyde, but at the same time they, being neither artists nor scientists, unlike Dr. Lanyon, cannot be allowed by the author to notice details.

3. Now if Stevenson makes Enfield and Utterson too commonplace and too plain, they will not be able to express even the vague discomfort Hyde causes them. On the other hand, the reader is curious not only about their reactions but he wishes also to see Hyde's face for himself.

4. But the author himself does not see Hyde's face clearly enough, and could only have it described by Enfield or Utterson in some oblique, imaginative, suggestive way, which, however,

would not be a likely manner of expression on the part of these stolid souls.

I suggest that . . . the only way to solve the problem is to have the aspect of Hyde cause in Enfield and Utterson not only a shudder of repulsion but also something else. I suggest that the shock of Hyde's presence brings out the hidden artist in Utterson.

LESLIE FIEDLER
(*NO! IN THUNDER*. 1963)

. . . The somber good man and the glittering rascal are both two and one; they war within Stevenson's single country and in his single soul.

In *Dr. Jekyll and Mr. Hyde,* which Stevenson himself called a *"fable"*—that is, a dream allegorized into a morality—the point is made explicit: "I saw that of the two natures that contended in the field of my consciousness, even if I could rightly be said to be either, it was only because I was radically both." It is the respectable and lonely Dr. Jekyll who gives life to the monstrous Mr. Hyde; and once good has given form to the ecstasy of evil, the good can only destroy what it has shaped by destroying itself. The death of evil requires the death of good. *Jekyll and Hyde* is a tragedy, one of the only two tragedies that Stevenson ever wrote; but its allegory is too schematic, too slightly realized in terms of fiction and character, and too obviously colored with easy terror to be completely convincing; while its explicit morality demands that evil be portrayed finally as an obvious monster.

EDWIN M. EIGNER
(*ROBERT LOUIS STEVENSON AND THE ROMANTIC TRADITION*, 1966)

Jekyll was wrong in attempting to segregate the two sides of his life, and he was even more wrong in glorifying the one side while

alternately condemning and indulging the other. His chemical
experiment is simply a logical extension of this treatment. It is by no
means a new departure. The Spencer Tracy movie . . . makes a
great deal of Jekyll's noble attempt to eradicate the evil in man's
nature, but Stevenson's Jekyll is at least as much interested in
freeing his evil nature from restraint as he is in giving scope to
the good in him. . . . According to Jekyll . . . each of the two
natures is dear to him, and he sees himself as "radically both." . . .
Thus Jekyll, far from wishing to end his double nature, is
attempting to make it permanent. He does not mean, at the
beginning at least, to reject either of his identifies. And when
Hyde, the evil nature, appears for the first time, the experiment
may be thought of as incomplete, but it should certainly not be
considered a failure. . . . Hyde does not appear purely evil in this
adventure, but he does seem to bring out all the cruelty and malice
in those who judge him. . . . Enfield, the bystanders, and the other
narrators are rejecting a part of themselves when they reject Hyde,
and the more strenuously they excise him, the more thoroughly
they come to resemble their notion of him, and the more pro-
foundly they are affected by the encounter.

MASAO MIYOSHI
(*THE DIVIDED SELF*, 1969)

The important men of the book,. . . are all unmarried, intel-
lectually barren, emotionally stifled, joyless. Nor are things much
different in the city as a whole. The more prosperous business
people fix up their homes and shops, but in a fashion without
chic. Houses give an appearance of "coquetry," and store fronts
invite one like "rows of smiling saleswomen" (Chapter 1). The
rather handsome town houses in the back streets of Dr. Jekyll's
neighborhood are rented out to all sorts—"map-engravers, architects, shady lawyers, and the agents of obscure enterprises"
(Chapter 2). Everywhere the fog of the dismal city is inescapable,
even creeping under the doors and through the window jambs

(Chapter 5). The setting hides a wasteland behind that secure and relatively comfortable respectability of its inhabitants. . . .

For the mastery of the book is the vision it conjures of the late Victorian wasteland, truly a de-Hyde-rated land unfit to sustain a human being simultaneously in an honorable public life and a joyful private one.

JORGE LUIS BORGES
(*BORGES ON WRITING*, 1973)

In "Borges and Myself" I am concerned with the division between the private man and the public man. In "The Watcher" I am interested in the feeling I get every morning when I awake and find that I am Borges. The first thing I do is think of my many worries. Before awakening, I was nobody, or perhaps everybody and everything—one knows so little about sleep—but waking up, I feel cramped, and I have to go back to the drudgery of being Borges. So this is a contrast of a different kind. It is something deep down within myself—the fact that I feel constrained to be a particular individual, living in a particular city, in a particular time, and so on. This might be thought of as a variation on the Jekyll and Hyde motif. Stevenson thought of the division in ethical terms, but here the division is hardly ethical. It is between the high and fine idea of being all things or nothing in particular, and the fact of being changed into a single man. It is the difference between pantheism—for all we know, we are God when we are asleep—and being merely Mr. Borges in New York.

IRVING SAPOSNIK
(*ROBERT LOUIS STEVENSON*, 1974)

Hyde is usually described in metaphors because essentially that is what he is: a metaphor of uncontrolled appetites, an amoral abstraction driven by a compelling will unrestrained by any moral halter. Such a creature is, of necessity, only figuratively describable; for his deformity is moral rather than physical. Purposely left vague, he is best described as Jekyll-deformed—dwarfish, stumping, ape-like—a frightening parody of a man unable to exist on the surface. He and Jekyll are inextricably joined because one without the other cannot function in society. As Hyde is Jekyll's initial disguise, so Jekyll is Hyde's refuge after the Carew murder. If Jekyll reflects respectability, then Hyde is his image "through the looking glass."

Hyde's literal power ends with his suicide, but his metaphorical power is seemingly infinite. Many things to his contemporaries, he has grown beyond Stevenson's story in an age of automatic Freudian response. As Hyde has grown, Jekyll has been overshadowed so that his role has shifted from culprit to victim. Accordingly, the original fable has assumed a meaning neither significant for the nineteenth century nor substantial for the twentieth. The time has come for Jekyll and Hyde to be put back together again.

STEPHEN HEATH
("PSYCHOPATHIA SEXUALIS:
STEVENSON'S *STRANGE CASE*," 1986)

What we can see in all this is Stevenson's closeness to his age. It is at the end of the nineteenth century that is begun and developed the scientific study of the human sexual. Stevenson's time is the time of the pioneer sexologists. *Strange Case of Dr. Jekyll and Mr. Hyde* is published in the same year as Krafft-Ebing's *Psychopathia Sexualis* whose initial recognition of "the incompleteness of our knowledge concerning the pathology of the sexual life" might be taken as an insight into the difficulty Stevenson has in his story. . . . Hysteria had served in the nineteenth century as the representation of women and of sexuality, the latter dealt with in the former. . . . Now at the end of the century Stevenson provides a text—perhaps *the* text—for the representation of men and ,sexuality, excluding women and so the sexual and so hysteria and then finding the only language it can for what is, therefore, the emergence of the hidden male: the animal, the criminal, *perversion*. Perversion is men's narrative and their story. When the masks of hysteria are down and the system of representation it keeps going wavers, that is what they say. Not that perversion *is* the word on male sexuality, simply there is no other representation, and this one, at least, offers a reconstruction from within a masculine world of that masculine world: perversion replaces and complements hysteria, positive to negative, maintaining male and female, man and woman, at whatever cost, as the terms of identity. A *psychopathia sexualis* is no psychoanalysis.

PATRICK BRANTLINGER AND RICHARD BOYLE
(*DR. JEKYLL AND MR. HYDE*
AFTER ONE HUNDRED YEARS, 1988)

. . . *Jekyll and Hyde* is totally lacking in explicit political themes. The allegorization prompted by Fanny apparently did not lead to any elaboration of its social content. Hyde is an emanation of Jekyll's "transcendental medicine" or of Stevenson's nightmare, rather than of either a social class system that spawned criminality or an imperial domination that had shackled Ireland for centuries. Whatever the "moral" of the story—and at first there was none—it has to do with good versus evil in the abstract, not with the politics or even the police of late-Victorian society. The novella's anachronistic style and ahistoricism help it to seem timeless and universal, while also obscuring the literary sleight of hand that sneaks Hyde into the heart of the respectable bourgeoisie. Jekyll's metamorphosis is a matter of certain unbelievable "powders," not of politics nor even of science. But the mass cultural format of the first edition promised topical reality enough to the "populace"—the same readers who would have responded to the newsboys whom Utterson hears "crying themselves hoarse along the footways: 'Special edition. Shocking murder of an M.P.'"

PETER K. GARRETT
(DR. JEKYLL AND MR. HYDE
AFTER ONE HUNDRED YEARS, 1988)

. . . a subversive or sceptical reading can rejoin and reinterpret the common sense. Like any popular tale of terror, *Jekyll and Hyde* exploits the drama of uncertain control, of mysterious threat, the struggle for mastery, and the spectacle of victimization. As Jekyll's triumphant discovery of "a new province of knowledge and new avenues to fame and power" leads to utter and terrifying loss of control, we recognize an appeal to impulses and anxieties more powerful than the tale's moral framework, to fantasies and fears of releasing desire from social restraints and responsibilities. Gothic fiction depends at least as much on producing such disturbance as on containing it; its characteristic complication of narrative form and multiplication of voices, whether in conflict or complementarity, always express the effort required to establish control of meaning and often suggest its uncertain success. The narrative of *Jekyll and Hyde* advances precisely through a series of such efforts, through Utterson's quest and Enfield's, Lanyon's, and Jekyll's narratives, and through the larger development of the mystery plot that includes them. To observe how the voices and positions of the tale shift and blur is to see how these efforts all fail. Like Jekyll, the tale releases a force that cannot be mastered—not because it simply overwhelms all resistance but because all efforts at resistance or containment themselves become further instances of its cruel logic.

RONALD R. THOMAS
(DR. JEKYLL AND MR. HYDE
AFTER ONE HUNDRED YEARS, 1988)

The breakdown of the conventions of characters in this text corresponds to a breakdown of narrative conventions as well. The absence of a coherent self here is joined to the absence of a coherent plot. The "case" is composed not of chapters but of ten disparate documents identified only as letters, incidents, cases, statements. These parts never succeed in becoming a whole story that makes sense out of events; like Jekyll's character, they fray into "elements" that have less and less connection. The first of the pieces of the case is auspiciously titled, "The Story of the Door." But the story referred to is called a "bad story" by its teller, Enfield, because it is "far from explaining" the mystery it raises. It is the first account we have of the actions of Mr. Hyde and yet in the story itself, Hyde is not even named. Enfield "can't mention" the name, he says, even "though it is one of the points of my story.". . . [I]n fact, the point of the story cannot be named because it has no single point. The personalities in it cannot be clearly connected to one another and the events in it cannot be explained. . . . The remainder of the text is merely a repetition of this "story" gone "bad." . . . We move through its secret door into a world where names cannot be named, points cannot be reached, stories cannot be told. . . . The psychological infirmities with which the text is manifestly concerned always express themselves as narrative infirmities in *Jekyll and Hyde* . . . .

WILLIAM VEEDER
(*DR. JEKYLL AND MR. HYDE*
AFTER ONE HUNDRED YEARS, 1988)

At stake in *Jekyll and Hyde* is nothing less than patriarchy itself, the social organization whose ideals and customs, transmissions of property and title, and locations of power privilege the male. Understanding the Fathers in *Jekyll and Hyde* is helped by seeing patriarchy both traditionally and locally: first in terms of its age-old obligations, then in terms of its immediate configuration in late-Victorian Britain. Traditionally the obligations of patriarchs are three: to maintain the distinctions (master-servant, proper-improper) that ground patriarchy; to sustain the male ties (father-son, brother-brother) that constitute it; and to enter the wedlock (foregoing homosexuality) that perpetuates it. Exclusion and inclusion are the operative principles. Men must distinguish the patriarchal self from enemies, pretenders, competitors, corruptors; and they must affiliate through proper bonds at appropriate times. What Stevenson devastatingly demonstrates is that patriarchy behaves exactly counter to its obligations.

ELAINE SHOWALTER
(*SEXUAL ANARCHY*, 1990)

Stevenson was the fin-de-siècle laureate of the double life. . . . In contrast to the way it has been represented in film and popular culture, *Jekyll and Hyde* is a story about communities of men. From the moment of its publication, many critics have remarked on the "maleness," even the monasticism, of the story. The characters are all middle-aged bachelors who have no relationships with women except as servants. Furthermore, they are celibates whose major emotional contacts are with each other and with Henry Jekyll. A female reviewer of the book [Julia Wedgewood] expressed her surprise that "no woman's name occurs in the book, no romance is even suggested in it." "Mr. Stevenson," wrote the critic Alice Brown [in 1895], "is a boy who has no mind to play with girls." The romance of Jekyll and Hyde is conveyed instead through men's names, men's bodies, and men's psyches. . . .

In the multiplication of narrative viewpoints that makes up the story, . . . one voice is missing: that of Hyde himself. We never hear his account of the events, his memories of his strange birth, his pleasure and fear. Hyde's story would disturb the sexual economy of the text, the sense of panic at having liberated an uncontrollable desire. Hyde's hysterical narrative comes to us in two ways: in the representation of his feminine behavior, and in the body language of hysterical discourse. . . . Hyde's reality breaks through Jekyll's body in the shape of his hand, the timbre of his voice, and the quality of his gait.

JOYCE CAROL OATES

(1990)

The visionary starkness of *The Strange Case of Dr. Jekyll and Mr. Hyde* anticipates that of Freud in such late melancholy meditations as *Civilization and ·Its Discontents* (1929–30): there is a split in man's psyche between ego and instinct, between civilization and "nature," and the split can never be healed. Freud saw ethics as a reluctant concession of the individual to the group, veneer of a sort overlaid upon an unregenerate primordial self. The various stratagems of culture—including, not incidentally, the "sublimation" of raw aggression by way of art and science—are ultimately powerless to contain the discontent, which must erupt at certain periodic times, on a collective scale, as war. Stevenson's quintessentially Victorian parable is unique in that the protagonist initiates his tragedy of doubleness out of a fully lucid sensibility—one might say a scientific sensibility. Dr. Jekyll knows what he is doing, and why he is doing it, though he cannot, of course, know how it will turn out. What is unquestioned throughout the narrative, by either Jekyll or his circle of friends, is mankind's fallen nature: sin is *original*, and *irremediable*. For Hyde, though hidden, will not remain so. And when Jekyll finally destroys him he must destroy Jekyll too.

Suggested Reading

BIOGRAPHY AND LETTERS

Balfour, Graham. *The Life of Robert Louis Stevenson*. New York: Charles Scribner's Sons, 1901.

Calder, Jenni. *R L S: A Life Study*. New York: Oxford Univ. Press, 1980.

McLynn, Frank. *Robert Louis Stevenson: A Biography*. New York: Random House, 1995.

Lapierre, Alexandra. *Fanny Stevenson: A Romance of Destiny*. New York: Graf, 1995.

The Letters of Robert Louis Stevenson. Ed. Bradford A. Booth and Ernest Mehew. New Haven: Yale Univ. Press, 1994.

CRITICISM

Robert Louis Stevenson: The Critical Heritage. Ed. Paul Maixner. London: Routledge and Kegan Paul, 1981.

Stevenson and Victorian Scotland. Ed. Jenni Calder. Edinburgh: Edinburgh Univ. Press, 1981.

The Definitive Dr. Jekyll and Mr. Hyde Companion. Ed. Henry Geduld. New York: Garland, 1983.

Dr. Jekyll and Mr. Hyde after One Hundred Years. Ed. William Veeder and Gordon Hirsch. Chicago: Univ. of Chicago Press, 1988.

See particularly:

> Patrick Brantlinger and Richard Boyle, "Stevenson's 'Gothic Gnome' and the Mass Readership of Late Victorian England."
>
> Peter K. Garrett, "Cries and Voices: Reading *Jekyll and Hyde*."
>
> Gordon Hirsch, "*Frankenstein,* Detective Fiction, and *Jekyll and Hyde*."
>
> Ronald R. Thomas, "The Strange Voices in the Strange Case: Dr. Jekyll, Mr. Hyde, and the Voices of Modern Fiction."
>
> William Veeder, "Questions of Text," and "Children of the Night: Stevenson and the Patriarchy."
>
> Virginia Wright Waxman, "Horrors of the Body: Hollywood's Discourse on Beauty and Rouben Mamoulian's Dr. Jekyll and Mr. Hyde."

Borges, Jorge Luis. *Borges on Writing.* Ed. Norman Thomas diGiovanni, Daniel Halpern, and Frank MacShane. New York: E. P. Dutton, 1973.

Brantlinger, Patrick. *The Reading Lesson: The Threat of Mass Literacy in Nineteenth-Century British Fiction.* Bloomington: Indiana Univ. Press, 1998.

Chesterton, G. K. *Robert Louis Stevenson.* New York: Dodd, Mead, 1928.

Cohen, Ed. "The Double Lives of Men: Narration and Identification in the Late Nineteenth-Century Representation of Ex-Centric Masculinities." *Victorian Studies* 36:3 (Spring 1993): 353–376.

Daiches, David. *Robert Louis Stevenson: A Revaluation.* Norfolk, CT: New Directions, 1947.

———. *Robert Louis Stevenson and His World*. London: Thames and Hudson, 1973.

Eigner, Edwin M. *Robert Louis Stevenson and Romantic Tradition.*Princeton: Princeton Univ. Press, 1966.

Fiedler, Leslie. *No! In Thunder.* London: Eyre and Spottiswoode, 1963.

Halberstam, Judith. *Skin Shows: Gothic Horror and the Technology of Monsters,* Durham, NC: Duke Univ. Press, 1995.

Heath, Stephen. "Psychopathia sexualis: Stevenson's *Strange Case.*" *Critical Quarterly* 28 (1986): 93–108.

Honaker, Lisa. *Revising Romance: Gender, Genre, and the Late-Victorian Anti-Realists.* New Brunswick, NJ: Rutgers Univ. Dissertation, 1993.

Hughes, Winifred. *The Maniac in the Cellar: Sensation Novels of the 1860s.* Princeton: Princeton Univ. Press, 1980.

Jackson, Rosemary. *Fantasy: The Literature of Subversion.* London: Methuen, 1981.

Kiely, Robert. *Robert Louis Stevenson and the Fiction of Adventure.* Cambridge, MA: Harvard Univ. Press, 1964.

Levine, George. *Darwin and the Novelists: Patterns of Science in Victorian Fiction.* Cambridge, MA: Harvard Univ. Press, 1988.

———. *The Realistic Imagination: English Fiction from Frankenstein to Lady Chatterley.* Chicago: Univ. of Chicago Press, 1981.

H. L. Malachow, *Gothic Images of Race in Nineteenth-Century Britain.* Stanford: Stanford Univ. Press, 1996.

Miller, Karl. *Doubles: Studies in Literary History*. New York: Oxford Univ. Press, 1985.

Miyoshi, Masao. *The Divided Self: A Perspective on the Literature of the Victorians*. New York: New York Univ. Press, 1969.

Nabokov, Vladimir. "The Strange Case of Dr. Jekyll and Mr. Hyde," in *Lectures on Literature*, ed. Fredson Bowers. New York: Harcourt Brace Jovanovich, 1980.

Saposnik, Irving S. *Robert Louis Stevenson*. New York: Twayne, 1974.

Oates, Joyce Carol. "Forward," *The Strange Case of Dr. Jekyll and Mr. Hyde*. Lincoln: Univ. of Nebraska Press, 1990.

Showalter, Elaine. *Sexual Anarchy: Gender and Culture at the* Fin de Siecle. New York: Viking, 1990.

Stewart, Garrett. *Dear Reader: The Conscripted Audience in Nineteenth-Century British Fiction*. Baltimore: Johns Hopkins Univ. Press, 1996.

Stone, Donald. *Novelists in a Changing World*. Cambridge, MA: Harvard Univ. Press, 1972.

Thomas, Ronald R. *Dreams of Authority: Freud and the Fictions of the Unconscious*. Ithaca: Cornell Univ. Press, 1990.

Twitchell, James B. *Dreadful Pleasures: An Anatomy of Modern Horror*. New York: Oxford Univ. Press, 1985.

Walkowitz, Judith. *City of Dreadful Delight: Narratives of Sexual Danger in Victorian London*. Chicago: Univ. of Chicago Press, 1992.

NOVEL

Martin, Valerie. *Mary Reilly: The Untold Story of Dr. Jekyll and Mr. Hyde.* New York: Simon and Schuster, 1990.

FILMS

Dr. Jekyll and Mr. Hyde, directed by John S. Robertson (1920), with John Barrymore and Nita Naldi.

Dr. Jekyll and Mr. Hyde, directed by Rouben Mamoulian (1932), with Fredric March, Miriam Hopkins, and Rose Hobart.

Dr. Jekyll and Mr. Hyde, directed by Victor Fleming (1941), with Spencer Tracy, Ingrid Bergman, and Lana Turner.